GIRL NEXT DOOR

A JACK RYDER NOVEL

WILLOW ROSE

Published by BUOY MEDIA LLC

Cover design by Juan Villar Padron,
https://www.juanjpadron.com

Special thanks to my editor Janell Parque
http://janellparque.blogspot.com/

To be the first to hear about new releases and bargains—from Willow Rose—sign up below to be on the VIP List. (I promise not to share your email with anyone else, and I won't clutter your inbox.)

- Sign up to be on the VIP LIST here :

http://bit.ly/VIP-subscribe

Tired of too many emails? Text the word: "willowrose" to 31996 to sign up to Willow's VIP text List to get a text alert with news about New Releases, Giveaways, Bargains and Free books from Willow.

Follow Willow Rose on BookBub:
https://www.bookbub.com/authors/willow-rose

Connect with Willow online:

- https://www.facebook.com/willowredrose
- www.willow-rose.net
- http://www.goodreads.com/author/show/4804769.Willow_Rose
- https://twitter.com/madamwillowrose
- madamewillowrose@gmail.com

BOOKS BY THE AUTHOR

MYSTERY/THRILLER/HORROR NOVELS

- In One Fell Swoop
- Umbrella Man
- Blackbird Fly
- To Hell in a Handbasket
- Edwina

MARY MILLS MYSTERY SERIES

- What Hurts the Most
- You Can Run
- You Can't Hide
- Careful Little Eyes

EMMA FROST SERIES

- Itsy Bitsy Spider
- Miss Dolly had a Dolly
- Run, Run as Fast as You Can
- Cross Your Heart and Hope to Die
- Peek-a-Boo I See You

- Tweedledum and Tweedledee
- Easy as One, Two, Three
- There's No Place like Home
- Slenderman
- Where the Wild Roses Grow
- Waltzing Mathilda
- Drip Drop Dead

JACK RYDER SERIES

- Hit the Road Jack
- Slip out the Back Jack
- The House that Jack Built
- Black Jack
- Girl Next Door
- Her Final Word
- Don't Tell

REBEKKA FRANCK SERIES

- One, Two...He is Coming for You
- Three, Four...Better Lock Your Door
- Five, Six...Grab your Crucifix
- Seven, Eight...Gonna Stay up Late
- Nine, Ten...Never Sleep Again

- Eleven, Twelve…Dig and Delve
- Thirteen, Fourteen…Little Boy Unseen
- Better Not Cry
- Ten Little Girls
- It Ends Here

HORROR SHORT-STORIES

- Mommy Dearest
- The Bird
- Better watch out
- Eenie, Meenie
- Rock-a-Bye Baby
- Nibble, Nibble, Crunch
- Humpty Dumpty
- Chain Letter

PARANORMAL SUSPENSE/ROMANCE NOVELS

- In Cold Blood
- The Surge
- Girl Divided

THE VAMPIRES OF SHADOW HILLS SERIES

- Flesh and Blood
- Blood and Fire
- Fire and Beauty
- Beauty and Beasts
- Beasts and Magic
- Magic and Witchcraft
- Witchcraft and War
- War and Order
- Order and Chaos
- Chaos and Courage

THE AFTERLIFE SERIES

- Beyond
- Serenity
- Endurance
- Courageous

THE WOLFBOY CHRONICLES

- A Gypsy Song
- I am WOLF

DAUGHTERS OF THE JAGUAR

- Savage
- Broken

Hell is empty

All the devils are here.

— - WILLIAM SHAKESPEARE, THE TEMPEST

We serial killers are your sons, we are your husbands, we are everywhere.

— - TED BUNDY

PROLOGUE

February 1974

"It was a perfect day. The air was crisp, the wind chilly as it blew from the north where they had a snowstorm. It didn't mean it got cold in Cocoa Beach; it just meant the air felt fresher and lighter than usual. It also meant I got to wear my jeans to school and the new hoodie that my mother had bought for me at the mall a couple of weeks ago. Everything up till this point was perfect. I couldn't wait to get home and tell my mother the great news. It never occurred to me that this would be the darkest day of my life.

"I remember how I clutched the envelope between my hands, feeling giddy with joy, thinking about the future.

"Full scholarship. A full ride.

"The words still clung in my head, as they had since they had fallen from my student counselor's mouth earlier in the day. I had barely been able to breathe inside his office as he showed me the letter containing the key to my future.

"My hard work had finally paid off.

"It had been a few tough years since we moved to Florida from Ohio two years ago. I wasn't used to hard times. I had always been a straight A-student. I had always been outgoing and easily made friends. But since the move, I had found myself a little off balance; it had been harder than I expected. My grades had slid slightly during my first year here, and no one seemed to want to be my friend. But over the past few months, things had been shaping up. I had made a few good friends, and my grades were back to where they used to be. It was just like my father had always told me: *All good things come to those who wait.* And then he would add: *and work hard. You have to work hard to get anything in this life.*

"Life hadn't been easy for my parents. Both came from poor backgrounds. But my father had worked his way up in the world. He had worked hard all his life to provide for my two younger siblings and me. Still, I had always known that they would never be able to afford for me to go to college. It was simply not doable.

"Until this very day. Until the counselor had called me out in the hallway and asked me to come into his office. A future leader, he called me when handing me the letter. As I walked home from school, I remember I still had that tickling sensation in the pit of my stomach just thinking about it.

"Mom is going to be so proud. No one has ever gone to college in our family before me.

"I hugged the letter and couldn't stop smiling when a girl from my street rode up behind me on her bike.

"'Hi, Steve.'"

"I turned briefly but continued to walk. The girl walked up next to me, pushing her bike.

"'Hi, Juanita,' I said.

"'What you got there?' she asked and looked at the envelope containing my letter.

"'Just a letter for my parents,' I said.

"I didn't want to tell anyone yet, especially not Juanita, whose parents would never be able to afford college for her either. I didn't want to rub it in her face. She lived across the street from us with her five siblings, and we both knew that once we graduated this summer, she was going to help out at her dad's restaurant and she would probably end up doing that until she married and had children. It was expected of her. Even though she was a genius at math. There was no way her dad would ever let her pursue anything else.

"'So, what did you get on your biology paper?' she asked, probably just trying to make conversation. I knew she liked me, but I had no time for girlfriends. Especially not now. I can't afford the distraction.

"'Let me guess. An A…as usual?' she said.

"I answered with a smile while still hugging the envelope. Juanita chuckled, and we stopped as we reached the entrance to my driveway.

"Juanita smiled too and was about to say something when she paused.

"'Say…isn't that your dog?'

February 1974

"I stared at the dog in the neighbor's yard. It was lifting its leg against their daughter's bike and relieving itself.

"'Dylan!' I yelled.

"The Doberman lifted his head and looked in my direction but didn't come to me even though I called. Who had let him out? I wondered. We never let Dylan out of the house alone. Not since he bit the Freidman's eight-year-old son from down the street. That was the third time the dog had bitten someone and, after that, my dad had told us not to let the dog out on its own again.

"'He must have escaped somehow,' I mumbled.

"I put my backpack down and put the envelope inside of it, to make sure nothing happened to it. Then I walked toward the dog in the neighbor's yard, hoping and praying they weren't home yet.

"Juanita put down her bike, and we approached the dog together. Dylan started growling as he saw us come closer.

"'Dylan,' I said, harshly. I needed to show it who was boss, my dad always said. 'Come here!'

"But the dog didn't budge. It walked across the grass and then squatted and relieved itself again, this time in a more solid manner.

"'Eeeww,' Juanita said, while I sighed, annoyed. I knew that I would have to pick it up before the neighbors came home. The neighbors hated our dog and always complained that it barked at night.

"'Come here, Dylan; you're coming home with me now,' I said and walked closer to the dog. I grabbed it by its collar and pulled it off the Hansons' lawn. Juanita came up to me, and Dylan let out a low growl when he saw her. I pulled the collar again to make it stop, but that just made the dog snap at her and Juanita pulled back with a light gasp.

"'I'm sorry,' I said. 'This dog is impossible. He doesn't like strangers.'

"'It's okay,' Juanita said and backed up a few steps further. 'I just wanted to help.'

"'I know,' I said. 'I've got him now. I'll take him home. He's lucky my dad won't be home till later or else he would face a bad beating. He knows he's not allowed outside on his own.'

"Juanita nodded. 'Okay. Guess I'll see you tomorrow then?'

"I forced a smile. 'Sure.'

"I watched Juanita grab her bike, then send me a soft smile before taking off toward her own house. As I watched her ride off, I wondered if things had been different if I would be able to like her back. She was ever so cute, and I really liked her eyes.

"In another place in time.

"'Come on, Dylan. Let's get you back inside the house before anyone complains. How did you escape anyway, huh? Maybe we should rename you the Great Houdini? Would you like th…?'

"I suddenly stopped talking. As I looked at my house, I realized the dog escaping wasn't the only thing odd on this crisp afternoon.

"The garage door was left open, and my mom's car was gone. To most people, that wouldn't be alarming, but to me it most certainly was. My mother was always home to greet my siblings and me when we came home from school.

"Always.

February 1974

"The first thing I noticed when stepping into the kitchen was a half-made peanut butter sandwich sitting on the counter next to an empty lunch box with my younger sister's name on the side.

"Baffled, I let go of Dylan and walked to the counter. The bread had gone hard on the edges, and the peanut butter that was only half spread on one side had dried up and sat in lumps. The knife was on the counter, still smeared in the brown substance that my sister loved so much, but I never took a liking to. It all gets a little blurry from there on, but I remember that I stared at the knife, dumbfounded, not sure what to believe. My heart rate was going up rapidly. My mom had clearly been making lunches for my siblings, but why hadn't she finished? Had something happened?

"'Mom?' I called out. I could hear my voice quivering as the sound was returned to me as an echo.

"'Mom?' I tried again, slightly shrill and anxiously.

"But there was no answer. Why was there no answer? My mom always answered when I called. You have to understand. She was always there.

"Always.

"'MO-OM!'

"I felt how my legs went soft and wobbly beneath me as fear set in. Desperately, I walked to the stairs, called my mother's name, then my siblings' one by one, and then my father's, even though I knew there was no way he was home already.

"But the thing was, his car had been in the garage, not my mother's.

"I wondered. Was something wrong with my dad's car? Had he maybe taken her car instead? Could it be as simple as that?

"'Dad?' I almost screamed.

"And that was when I saw the blood. There was

blood on the floor and up the stairs. I stared at it, my hands beginning to shake, while the dog took off. It sprinted up the stairs like someone had told it to go find a treat up there somewhere.

"I followed. I walked up the steps, my legs heavy and my hands trembling. As I reached the top of the stairs, I heard my dog whimpering, half growling. I then rushed into my parents' bedroom. In there, I first spotted Dylan on the bed; then I saw what the dog had in his mouth. He was pulling at it. The sight made me want to scream.

"It was my mother's arm.

"'DYLAN!' I yelled, then rushed to get the dog away from my mother, who was lying on the mattress. The dog let go, then backed up while I walked closer to better see what was wrong with my mother.

"I stared at the face behind the plastic bag, and the first thing I noticed was that it wasn't moving. The bag remained completely still, as were my mother's eyes.

"I turned my head and spotted my father's body on the carpet behind the bed. It was lying there just as still as my mother's, a belt wrapped around his throat, his face bloated and grotesquely swollen.

Both of them had been bound with thin cords at the wrists and ankles.

"I wanted to move. I wanted to do something, to pull the darn bag off my mother's head, but I couldn't. I was frozen in place. It was like I was trapped in a nightmare, but no matter how hard I tried to wake up, it didn't happen. I wanted to scream, to yell at my mother to get up, to take the bag off and stop playing games, that it wasn't funny, it was some cruel, cruel joke. I wanted to call to my dad to rise to his feet and stand up straight. But no sound left my lips. No part of my body would obey. Fear had me fixed to the ground. I couldn't move.

"Not until I heard a noise. It was coming from my brother's bedroom next door. I stopped breathing as I realized that someone was in the house.

February 1974

"My pulse was like a heavy drum in my ears, drowning out everything else. I stormed out of the bedroom and slipped as I headed for the stairs. The perpetrator was coming up behind me. I grabbed the railing and rushed down the stairs, taking two steps at a time. Behind me, I could hear the perpetrator. I could hear the breathing, and I was certain I could even hear laughter.

"Get to the door, Steve, I remember thinking. *Just get out into the street and scream for help. Juanita might still be out there, or someone else.*

"The perpetrator behind me was closing in. I raced down the stairs, hearing the heavy breathing behind me as the person closed the gap, reached out a hand, and grabbed me by the hoodie. I was forcefully jerked backward, and the air was pushed out of my throat. I landed with my back against the steps and heard the sound of something cracking, followed by pain. As I lay there screaming, I opened my eyes and looked into those of the person holding me down. The face was covered with a doll's mask, picturing a woman with rosy red lips, light pink skin, and black painted eyebrows. The mask had deep holes where the eyes peeked out. Big steel grey eyes.

"Like those of a wolf.

"I screamed again as a fist was raised and slammed down on my face, each punch followed by a deep laugh.

"'HEEELP!'

"More punches fell, and soon I tasted blood in my mouth and my vision became blurred. I felt dizzy and could barely stay conscious. The blows stopped, and I felt myself being dragged up the stairs, the back of my head bumping onto each step, causing the pain in my back to flare up, but having no strength to scream or even moan anymore. The bumping continued till it suddenly stopped and everything went quiet for a little while. The next thing I heard was the sound of something coming closer and, as I opened my eyes again and watched through patches of blood, I realized I was now looking out through a plastic bag.

"Oh, dear God, no!

"I tried to move, to fight the man off as he closed the bag using a cord around my throat. The bag moved back and forth against my skin as I fought to breathe. The inside of it soon turned foggy while I felt the perpetrator fumbling behind me, trying to tie up my arms. It was through that fog that I spotted another set of eyes staring back at me. The very familiar brown eyes of my dog.

"Dylan!

"I had no air to scream at the dog, and there was no need for it. The black Doberman exposed his teeth, let out a loud snarl, then went directly for the perpetrator's thigh. I could hear as the teeth went through the jeans and sunk into the skin and I could have sworn I even heard the bone crushing as the dog bit down. The perpetrator let out a loud roar and turned to hit the dog, but Dylan didn't move an inch. While I reached up my hands to pull off the plastic bag and dash for the stairs, Dylan held onto the thigh with all the strength he had in him, and as I raced for the door, reaching out for the door handle, I knew I would be forever indebted to the darn dog.

"Behind me, I heard the dog whimper loudly, and then followed the sound of fast moving steps on the stairs. Realizing the perpetrator had somehow fought off Dylan, I was spurred into motion. I sprang into the driveway, gravel skidding beneath my feet. Screaming for help, I ran into the street, tripped on a lawn sprinkler and landed in the grass, face first, having the air knocked out of me. Behind me, the door was yanked open. I scrambled to my feet and turned my head with a gasp. My eyes searched frantically behind me and met the steel grey ones behind the mask before I ran into the street, screaming for help. The sound of feet behind me on the asphalt made me run even faster down the street till I reached the river and plunged into the brown water. Luckily, I am an excellent swimmer, and I stayed under the murky water for as long as I could without breathing, then swam for the dock at the Williams' house. I swam underneath it, grabbed onto the wood, and stayed like that for hours, continually staring at the water behind me, wondering if the perpetrator had taken up the chase and plunged into the water as well. I was just waiting for that doll mask to appear out of the murky water.

“It was dark before I dared to climb up onto the dock and run into the Williams’ backyard and knock on their sliding doors. The rest of the story, you know."

Steve stopped talking and exhaled deeply, feeling how his mouth had grown dry. He wiped a couple of tears from his cheeks and held onto the table to stop his hands from shaking.

The man in front of Steve nodded. He wrote a few words on his pad, then looked up at him. Steve took a sip of water and swallowed. The man took off his glasses and put them on the table in front of him. He grabbed the recorder on the table and turned it off.

"Thank you, Steve. I think I have what I need."

Steve sighed. Telling his story always drained him. It didn't matter if it was the police, a psychologist, or journalists who asked him to. It was so painful to go back there again and again.

"So, when will it be in the paper?" he asked.

"Tomorrow. It's our front-cover story."

Steve nodded, tired. He was about to start

crying again but held it back. He was getting quite good at that. He couldn't allow himself to get carried away. Crying wouldn't get him anywhere.

"Good," he said with a sniffle. "I just want the world to know what this bastard has done and warn anyone else to be careful."

"I know you do. And we appreciate it greatly. You are very brave to come forward like this and I know it hurts terribly to tell your story, but you did a great job."

Steve exhaled. "Maybe this way the bastard will get caught and people can get back to sleeping peacefully again. That's all I can pray for. I just want justice for my family. I want this monster to get caught."

The journalist rose to his feet and gathered his things. He reached out his hand and shook Steve's.

"That's what I pray for too."

PART ONE

CHAPTER ONE

August 2018

It was a busy street, yet no one saw the young boy as he leaped into it. Maybe it was because they didn't expect a young boy to run into A1A like that during rush-hour, without looking for cars. Or perhaps they were just too busy to notice, going to their jobs or other destinations only the drivers themselves knew.

A woman did see him, though. Old Mrs. McMullen was standing on the other side of the four-lane road, where the car rushed past at forty-five miles an hour, while most of them were going fifty-five. She was out walking her dog, her four-month-old Standard Schnauzer, Fluffy, that her son-in-law had gotten for her, picked up at some breeder half an hour from where she lived in her beachside community. Fluffy didn't see anything and, at first, old Mrs. McMullen believed she had to be mistaken, that she was imagining things, maybe seeing things that weren't even there. It wasn't the first time, you know. She was suffering from worsening Alzheimer's that made her forget and sometimes even see things that weren't really there. At least, that's what her children told her.

Mrs. McMullen blinked a few times, but the boy was still there in the middle of the road, zigzagging between the cars, not looking where he was going.

Old Mrs. McMullen shouted. A loud piercing cry, but it was completely drowned out by the roars coming from the cars.

The boy ran between the cars like he was confused where to go, but also like he didn't even realize where he was, and they missed him by a hair, much to the old woman's relief.

But then he stopped.

The boy stood in the middle of the road and, right before the car hit him, he turned his face toward Mrs. McMullen like had he finally heard her screams, and their eyes met.

It was a moment she was certain not even the Alzheimer's would be able to erase from her mind.

CHAPTER TWO

August 2018

The Weasel walked through the police tape when Sergeant Mike Wagner approached her. The house in front of her was a typical old Cocoa Beach beach-house. Three bedrooms, two and a half baths. Small kitchen, small backyard with a shed—probably used for surfboards—and a hammock between the palm trees.

"So, what are we looking at?" she asked. They had briefed her on the phone, but she needed to hear it one more time. With more details.

"Double homicide. A woman in her mid-thirties and her daughter, eleven years old."

"And they're related to the boy?" she asked and walked to the front door, putting on gloves that

Mike handed her. The forensics team hadn't arrived yet, and she had to be very careful not to contaminate the scene.

"Yes. They're his mom and sister," Mike said.

Weasel walked into the living room where the body of the mother lay on the floor. Her eyes were wide open on the severed head that lay inches from the body. Her hands and feet were tied with cords. The Weasel drew in a deep breath, then nodded.

They had received the call this morning about a fifteen-year-old boy, Parker Reynolds, who had run into A1A in the middle of rush hour traffic and then gotten himself hit by a car. He was then slung through the air and hit by another car before they finally managed to stop. The scene had been a mess, but the boy was still alive. Barely, though. He was now in the hospital in Cape Canaveral, where they were fighting for his life. As soon as they had identified the boy, her officers had set out to notify the family, but as they arrived, they had found the mother and sister dead.

"And the husband?"

"Not in the picture as far as we know," Mike said. "They're separated. He lives down in Palm Bay. He's been notified and is on his way here."

"That should give us a quick ID, then. Where's the girl?"

"The bedroom. In the back."

Weasel nodded and walked down the hallway. Pictures of the girl and her brother hung on the wall from when they were just young children. Next to the bathroom were pencil marks on the wall with their different heights next to dates and years.

Not gonna be any more of those, Weasel thought to herself morbidly.

"In here?" she asked and pointed at the door with the many KEEP OUT and KNOCK FIRST signs. Mike nodded.

Weasel stepped inside, then gasped. Tears appeared in her eyes, but she didn't give into them. Her heart pounded in her chest as she stared at the lifeless girl dangling from the ceiling above her bed, her face barely visible behind the plastic bag. On the floor stood a backpack next to her lunch bag. She had been getting ready to go to school. Mike came up behind her.

"He used her own belt to hang her with."

Weasel swallowed the lump in her throat. "I see."

Mike stood next to her, and she fought to hold

back tears. As the head of the police department, she couldn't show emotions in a situation like this.

"So, what do we do next?" Mike asked.

"I guess we call in Ryder," she said. "He'll know how to handle this. If anyone can, it's him."

CHAPTER THREE

August 2018

"Here you go. The house is all yours."

Mary Hass, the realtor who had been helping Diane find a new place to live, dangled the keys in front of Diane's face. Diane grabbed them with a happy chuckle. They were standing on the porch of the small bungalow style white painted beach house in North Cocoa Beach.

Diane lifted her head but remained silent.

"What?" Mary said. "You're not going inside?"

"I'm just listening," Diane said. "I can hear the ocean."

"It is literally just one block away," Mary said. "Imagine going down there every morning for a quick swim or after work when you're all sweaty and gross. Nothing beats the ocean."

Diane took in a deep breath and smelled the fresh air being brought to her porch by the breeze coming from the ocean. It smelled divine.

"Thank you," she said. "Without you, I would never have found this little pearl of a house."

"You were lucky," Mary said and looked at her phone. "No one gets a house for that price around here. A condo maybe. But not a three-bedroom three bath, no way."

"Guess luck is finally smiling on me," Diane mumbled.

Mary was still looking at her phone, her finger sliding across the screen. "Yes, well. Congratulations. Enjoy your new house." She lifted her phone up, then took a selfie with Diane. "For the Facebook page," she said and tapped on the screen afterward. "We like to do a little post every time we make a deal. You know, to show business is booming and all that."

"Of course," Diane said and looked at the keys in her hand.

"*Anywh-o-o*, enjoy your new home and let me know if you're ever in the market for an upgrade."

"Thank you."

Diane waved at Mary as she rushed to her car, her nose once again stuck in the phone, even as she put the key in the ignition and rushed off down the street.

When she was finally gone, Diane took in another deep breath of the fresh air, then put the key in the door and opened it. The musty smell that met her was no surprise, since she had been to the house several times before and knew it had been empty for many years. This was what you'd call a fixer-upper, or what people like Mary would call a *home of great potential, with lots of curb appeal,* but that didn't frighten Diane one bit. Even if she never got it fixed up properly, she knew she could make a good home for herself and Misty, her cat. She didn't need granite countertops to be happy. She didn't need IKEA furniture or a flat screen TV. She was happy to simply have a roof over her head, one that was safe.

Diane walked to her small Toyota and grabbed Misty in her arms. The cat complained slightly. Diane brought him inside and put him down on the old wooden floors. The cat immediately took off, sniffing his way around the kitchen.

"There you go, buddy. Get comfortable. I know I will. This is our new home. This is where we start over again, just the two of us."

CHAPTER FOUR

August 2018

"Registration day is tomorrow?"

I looked at my twins, Abigail and Austin with wide eyes. Tyler—my very energetic two-year-old was sitting in my lap, playing with my phone, giving me a much-deserved break.

Abigail rolled her eyes. "We told you this yesterday. You're the one who's supposed to keep track of these things, not us."

I sighed, exhausted. I had been alone with the kids all summer while my wife, Shannon King, the world-famous country singer, was on tour. It was sort of her comeback tour, one of those you can't miss even if you have six kids in the house. Granted, only two of them were hers, but still. She had left me alone in a madhouse and wasn't coming back for six more weeks.

I wasn't sure I was going to make it.

"All right then. So, we go get you kiddos registered tomorrow and meet your teachers."

I smiled, not at them, but because this meant they would go back to school in just a few days. With Tyler in pre-school, that meant things could finally get back to normal. I wouldn't have to depend so much on my parents helping me out whenever I needed to work. I would occasionally leave them alone with Emily in charge, but I wasn't too fond of doing that. She was nineteen now but had been through a couple of rough years. I didn't want to impose too much responsibility on her shoulders. Handling three nine-year-olds, one twelve-year-old, and also a two-year-old was too much for her. I was so grateful that I had my parents living close by.

While Tyler played with the phone between his chubby hands, it started to ring. A picture of Shannon showed up, and Tyler shrieked with joy.

"Mommy!"

"Here, let me get that," I said and took the phone out of his hands, then picked it up.

"Hi, honey?" she chirped. "How are things back at the house?"

I looked around our newly-built beach house. It looked like a disaster. Toys were spread everywhere on the wooden floors. Someone had painted on the white walls next to the fridge with permanent marker. The girls had been making slime in the living room and left stains all over the couches and on the carpet.

"Mommy, Mommy, Mommy," Tyler whined and tried to grab the phone from my hand.

"Is that Tyler?" Shannon said. "Put him on."

I gave the boy the phone, and he shrieked with joy as he placed it against his ear. "Mommy?"

They spoke for a few minutes. It was mostly Shannon who did the talking, while Tyler just made babbling noises. After a few minutes, he lost interest and put the phone down on the counter while I could still hear Shannon talking to him.

"How about that, buddy, huh?"

"It's me again. I'm back. Tyler had somewhere to be," I said and watched as the young boy climbed down and staggered toward the living room, holding a wooden spoon in his hand that he without a doubt would use to hit one of his siblings with within the next few minutes and then they would come crying to me. At least I had a few minutes before it broke loose. A few minutes were all I needed to talk to my beloved wife.

"How are things, for real?" she asked.

"Tumultuous, would that be a word?" I asked.

"I am sorry," she said. "I feel bad."

"Don't. That won't help me one bit. Enjoy it, and I'll feel like it was all worth it."

I sighed and found my cup of coffee from this morning. I sipped it. It was cold, but I didn't care. Anything would do at this point.

"Don't forget registration day tomorrow," she said after a small pause.

"I'm on top of it," I said. "Everything is under control."

"Phew," she said. "So, I don't have to ask if you bought back-to-school supplies and clothes either?"

My eyes grew wide, and I almost spit out the cold coffee. I coughed instead. "Supplies? Clothes?"

"Oh, no, please tell me you've bought them?" she asked.

"No…no, of course, I have. As I said, I'm on top of it all. You don't have to worry about a thing."

I tried to sound reassuring. It worked.

"Of course, I don't. I am sorry I doubted you

for a second. Of course, you have it all under control. You're Jack Ryder, the perfect husband and father."

"Don't forget detective," I said.

"Of course not. Detective too. How's the new job?"

I looked out the window at the ocean in front of me. This house had the most gorgeous views of the Atlantic Ocean, and I kept forgetting to enjoy it because of all the busyness around me. One day I'd get to surf again, I thought. One day.

I had taken a transfer from the Brevard County Sherriff's office to the Cocoa Beach Police department. I needed a change of scenery and was sick of the commute. Cocoa Beach Police department was like coming home for me, and the position was brand new, so I wouldn't have to follow in anyone's footsteps. According to the Weasel, who was the chief of police there, I could take care of my own hours and even work from home from time to time if that was needed, which it most certainly was. It was a slight step down career-wise, since the area we covered was smaller and the cases a lot less attractive, coming from covering the entire county to only a small town with barely ten thousand inhabitants, but it was what I needed right now. I needed to slow down a little in order not to lose myself completely between my family and my work schedule.

"It's okay. Got a new case yesterday though. Ugly one. A mom and her daughter murdered in their own home right before they left for school and work. The son got out and got away but was struck by a car on A1A. Yesterday was busy, but my parents have been great at helping out. I've told Weasel I might do a lot of work from home, if possible, and she doesn't seem to mind. She knows I have a lot on my plate."

"I do like that woman," Shannon said. "Without her, I don't know how we would make things work."

"Neither do I," I said when I heard the expected scream coming from the living room, and less than a second later Angela stood in the doorway, holding the wooden spoon in one hand and Tyler in the other.

"Listen, honey; I need to go now. There's trouble."

"All right. I have a show tonight, and then we'll be on the road again tomorrow. Talk to you later."

I hung up with a deep exhale.

"He hit me," Angela said. Then added while holding the spoon up, "With this."

"I know. I'm sorry but listen up. Could you go get the others? We have some shopping we need to do, fast."

CHAPTER FIVE

It isn't that impossible in this society, and I know that there are many more out there like me, hiding in plain sight. I know because I have lived as an ordinary person all my life and I still do. Even though I have been living a parallel and increasingly sick life. But I have always managed to keep it to myself. It's not like I can put a finger on a certain date in my life and say that on that date I decided to be a killer. I think you are one way before you do the actual deed. For me, it was something that built up inside of me over the years, from my childhood and into adulthood. I was raging inside. My rage contained such incredible energies. Yet people would say that I was a nice guy. Sure, I looked troubled at times; I looked moody, but generally, if you asked people back then, they'd all say I was a nice guy. They liked me. But that was only because they didn't know what was really going on inside of me because I am very good at hiding it.

It was while growing up that I realized something dark was growing inside me and, even as I suppressed it, I knew one day it would demand my attention. As the years passed, it became more and more demanding and, finally, one day, I simply had to give in.

I had to do it.

I still remember the smell of his last breath. Of course, I do. He was, after all, my first kill. It was a surprise. He was a surprise. The fact that he was home was. I hadn't expected him to be. Knowing this family and their routine, having carefully planned this for months, I hadn't expected the father to be home. But he was, and that threw me out of balance at first. Of course, it did. He was strong, and he fought bravely for his family and for his own life. But I was stronger. As I wrapped the belt around his neck and tightened it, his face almost exploded. It swelled up so terribly, that's what I thought it would do.

I came in through the back door. I opened the unlocked door leading to the kitchen and let the dog out first. I knew it tended to bite, but as it realized it could run out freely, it no longer worried about me. It ran happily into the backyard where it had spotted a black raven to chase into a tree.

I heard voices coming from the kitchen as I stood in the doorway, the knife clutched between my fingers. It was morn-

ing. They were all going through their usual routines. The kids were upstairs getting ready, fighting over some toy, while their mother yelled at them to hurry up.

She was making their lunches as I entered. I was sweating behind the mask, and a droplet landed in my eye and stung. It wasn't that hot out since it was February, so I guess it was just my excitement that made me break into a sweat. This was, after all, my first. I was a virgin up until then. This was the culmination of many years of fantasizing and dreaming about doing this. Years of planning. And it was so perfect.

The woman didn't notice me at first as I moved in closer from behind her. She was smearing peanut butter on toast. She seemed stressed and was mumbling to herself. I stood there for what must have been a few seconds, a thrill of emotions rushing through me in waves, causing the hairs to rise on my arm.

Then she yelled. Still without turning around, holding a piece of toast in her hand, the butter knife in the other.

"Timothy! Brianna! Bus will be here soon. Come down now! Eat breakfast."

Timothy. Brianna. Those were the names of the two youngest in the family. Eight and ten years old when it happened.

When I happened.

"Coming!" a voice replied from up the stairs. It was Brianna's.

Then the woman went back to mumbling. I walked closer to her and could almost smell her. I imagined me reaching over and slicing her throat, killing her instantly just like that, but then regretted it. I remember thinking I wanted my first kill to be spectacular, and not fast. I wanted her to fight for her life. I guess I got what I wanted because, as I stood there, with the knife in my hand, ready to jump the woman, a voice interrupted me and threw me off guard.

The yelling was angry.

"Who are you? What are you doing in my house?"

I turned to look into the face of the father of the family. As I said, it took me completely off guard since the dad usually had left for work at this point of the day. I had studied their routines closely, as I do with all my victims, and the husband wasn't supposed to be there. Needless to say, I don't like surprises very much.

CHAPTER SIX

August 2018

"Ten minutes, Shannon!"

Shannon King nodded with a sigh as the door was closed again and the stage manager disappeared. She turned to look at herself in the mirror in front of her. Her make-up was on; her hair was set. She was ready for her next performance. Every night meant a new town.

"Where are we again?" she asked.

Sarah, her PA, looked up at her from her phone. "Detroit."

Shannon nodded. "Right."

She had brought Sarah along on her tour and was so grateful to have her with her. Without her to keep track of her life, she would probably go insane. Shannon corrected a lock of hair.

"How do I look?"

Sarah put the phone on the table and stood up. On the table was an immeasurable amount of chocolate boxes and flowers that Shannon would never even get to enjoy. It was the same everywhere she went. Sometimes, she wondered if she should have her manager call ahead and tell them to save the money they used on flowers and chocolate and donate them to some charity instead. It always filled Shannon with such deep guilt to look at all of it and know that it was just a waste.

"You want water before you go on?" Sarah asked.

"Yes, please," Shannon said, and Sarah went to the mini-fridge to grab one for her. Shannon took it and drank greedily without ruining her make up that her make-up artist had carefully smeared on her half an hour ago. Shannon felt a shooting pain in her hand as she put the bottle down and winced.

"Still bothering you, huh?" Sarah said. "Maybe you should have a doctor take a look at it again soon. It happened two years ago; it shouldn't still be bothering you."

"I'm okay," Shannon said and turned away.

She looked at her guitar in the corner and knew in a few seconds she would have to grab it. Shannon sighed. Holding the guitar used to be her joy; it used to make her feel so whole, but lately, it had filled her with despair instead. The pain in her hand was terrible when she was holding the guitar and playing made it even worse. It had been tolerable at home and almost didn't bother her until she went on the tour and had to play every day. The situation wasn't getting any better, and even though she tried hard to ignore it, she would soon have to admit that something was terribly wrong. Every night, when she came off stage, it hurt so badly it would keep her awake at night.

She had been injured in Savannah, where she and Jack had been married two years ago. A woman, actually Shannon's own deranged aunt, had taken Tyler, and she had fought her with the result that her hand was stabbed. The doctors had told her the pain would go away eventually, but so far, it seemed only to get worse. Shannon had thought about seeing a specialist, but there didn't seem to be much time in her life. Or maybe she was just terrified of the outcome. What if they told her she needed surgery? She wouldn't be able to perform. What if they said she would never be able to play her guitar again?

"You sure you're okay?" Sarah asked, concerned.

Shannon took in a deep breath, then grabbed the guitar, pressing the pain back and forcing a smile.

"Yes. And if you'll excuse me, I have a show to do."

Sarah smiled back, a sense of relief rushing over her face. "Break a leg."

CHAPTER SEVEN

Cocoa Beach 2007

He was the most amazing man in the world, his father. He wasn't handsome—at least mom said he wasn't—but he was big. Tall and strong, so strong that the boy was certain he had to be the strongest man in the entire world, maybe even the universe. Standing six foot eight and two hundred and fifty pounds, the boy had to bend his neck all the way back as far as he could even to look up at him and see his face.

And he did just that, look up to him in every way possible. Everything his father did was awesome. Especially when he was fixing the car, and the boy helped by bringing him the tools he asked for. Those were the most amazing moments of his entire childhood. If he fixed the drain in the kitchen or the bathroom, it was the most incredible thing in the world for the boy. To just watch his dad as he grunted and groaned, used the tools to make things better for Mom.

And as his dad explained to him early on, that's what it was all about. Making Mom happy and hopefully keeping her that way. Because if she was happy, then they all were.

So, the boy tried his best to make her happy as well, even though it was a tough job. More often than not, she would yell at both him and his dad for not doing things properly. Like for making a mess or for dragging in dirt with their shoes. Or for eating with their mouths open, or for leaving the lights on in the bathroom, or for dragging their feet across the floors. Anything they might do wrong. Which, apparently, was a lot, whereas his baby sister apparently could do nothing wrong. Not even when she kept all of them awake at night by crying and screaming.

And the boy watched as his dad just took the yelling and never even tried to yell back. Not even once. The boy didn't understand why his dad didn't even try and defend himself, especially when Mom yelled at him for not having emptied the dishwasher when she had just asked him to clean up the garage. Or even worse when she would tell him he wasn't holding baby sister correctly and pull her out of his hands. She would call him irresponsible and all sorts of bad names that the boy didn't like.

But dad just took the yelling and so did the boy. Because that's what they did, the men of the house. Every now and then, the boy would see his dad clench his fist while the yelling happened, and once he even did it so hard that blood dripped from the palm of his hands onto the carpet from the wounds where his nails had dug in.

But he took the yelling. He stood there and took it, and that was how the boy learned to do the same. He learned how to bite down on his lip to not talk back at her because that would only make her even angrier. Even though it meant the boy constantly had sores on his lips from biting them. Sores that would hurt at night when he went to sleep, waiting for his mom to tuck him in like she used to do before his little sister came into their world, but she never had time to anymore.

"You're a big boy now," she had told him a few weeks after the baby was born. She had said the words without stroking his hair or kissing him gently on the forehead like she usually did. "Big boys don't need their mommas so much anymore."

The boy had then asked his dad if being a big boy and four years old meant his mother didn't want him anymore, but his dad replied that Mommy was just exhausted from taking care of the baby, that was all.

"It'll get better for all of us once the baby is a little older. Until then, we men must make sure to take care of everything else around here, okay?"

"Okay," the boy had answered firmly, pressing back the tears piling up in his eyes. If there was one thing he knew about being a big boy, it was that they didn't cry.

CHAPTER EIGHT

August 2018

The line to get into the school was ridiculous. We all had to go through the front office if we wanted to walk our kids to class on the first day of school. And most of us had to since we were carrying huge bags of supplies that the children couldn't carry themselves. I had an extra reason, and her name was Betsy Sue. She had never been in school before, and I wanted to walk her to the classroom to make sure she was all right and that she would get the best possible start to the school year. The three A's, Austin, Abigail, and Angela knew their way around, but for Betsy Sue, this had to be a shock of monumental proportions. Up until now, she had lived her entire life inside a crazy woman's house after being kidnapped as just an infant. The past two years, Shannon and I had hired a private teacher for her to bring her up to speed with the other kids and ease her into her new life, but now we had decided it was time for her to go to a real school along with the other children. And Betsy Sue seemed to agree. She was looking forward to meeting the other kids. She would begin sixth grade, the last year of elementary school. I had already spoken to the school about her situation, and they were going to take really good care of her, they had promised me.

A sign on the side of the fence asked us to donate to the Alondra Browning Foundation, and the sight of it made my heart skip a beat. Alondra Browning was a young girl who was killed before the summer break when ten little girls had gone missing from Roosevelt Elementary. Unluckily, one of them had ended up in a body bag. I had handled the case for Cocoa Beach Police, and it was after that tragedy that they realized they needed my help fulltime. They needed someone like me on their team, Weasel had said when asking me to take the position.

"Welcome back. Ready for a new school year?" the lady behind the counter asked as she took my driver's license and scanned it. She was new, and on her name tag, it said, Mrs. Meyer.

"Not really," Abigail answered her. "I already miss the pool."

"I am kind of looking forward to a new year," Austin said.

He received a look from his twin sister. "Why do you have to be such a dork?"

"Am not," Austin said.

"So are," Abigail argued.

"All right, that's enough," I said, knowing how the two of them could go on for hours on end. Especially Abigail who never got out of the way of a good argument. Like me, Austin hated arguing and usually would just agree to anything his sister said, but I was beginning to see a new tendency in him as he was starting to speak up for himself more lately. It was a development I welcomed since I didn't want him to be run over by his dominating sister constantly, but it also meant a lot more fighting in our house and I, for one, couldn't wait to get the both of them shoved into the school and leave without them. Tyler was fussing and wanted me to pick him up, but I couldn't since I also had to carry all the supplies. Angela and Betsy Sue were both behaving so nicely as usual. Betsy Sue was holding a small coin in between her fingers that a raven had brought to her outside while we were waiting. It didn't happen as often as it used to, but she still had a way with those birds, just as she still talked to ghosts and believed that her friend Billy the ghost with the yellow skin had moved down with us when we brought her from Savannah. I had a feeling she just needed him to stay with her to make her feel safe and to have someone to blame things on if she had done something wrong.

The doctor had told us she would eventually let him go, once she felt more at home here, but after two years, he was apparently still with us, and I had to be careful where I sat down at the house since she would often scream and tell me I had sat on top of him.

The door buzzed open. "All right, kiddos. You're on your own," I said.

"Me first," Abigail said and rushed to the door and opened it first, Austin right behind her. They stormed into the hallway, yelling loudly, and I just knew they were going to get yelled at on the first day. I wondered if that was some sort of record.

"All right, Angela, you know where you need to go, and Betsy Sue, you come with Tyler and me. We'll walk you to your classroom after we drop off all the supplies."

CHAPTER NINE

August 2018

"Hi there. Welcome to the neighborhood."

The woman, who had stopped in front of Diane's house, sniffled and reached out her hand. Diane was sitting in a chair on her porch when she walked by.

"My name is Jean. I live a couple of houses down the street. Number two-thirteen."

"I'm Diane," she said and shook Jean's hand.

"So, you just moved in, huh?" Jean said.

Diane wiped sweat from her forehead. She was dirty and gross from the intensive cleaning.

"Yes."

"You renting?"

Diane shook her head and sipped from her water bottle. She couldn't stop sweating. She wasn't really used to this type of heat anymore.

"Nope. Bought the place."

Jean looked surprised. "You bought it. Really?"

"Yes, I know it doesn't look like much, but I think I can make a decent home of it."

Jean looked at the house, then back at Diane. She was holding a Yeti cup in her hand, and Diane suddenly noticed her breath smelled a little like alcohol. Diane pulled back so that she wouldn't smell it.

"If you say so," Jean said, grinning.

"I do. Me and Misty—that's my cat—will create a nice home for ourselves here."

Jean sipped from her Yeti, then nodded. "I am sure you will. Well, I just wanted to welcome you to the neighborhood."

"That's awfully ni…" Diane stopped talking as a car pulled up to the curb and the window was rolled down. A man wearing a uniform stuck his head out. He seemed tall even though he was sitting down.

"Hi there."

"This is Dennis Woods," Jean said. "He lives right across the street from you with his wife

Camille and two boys, whose names I don't remember. What are they again?"

"Lucas and Trenton," he said and kept looking at Diane. It made her slightly uncomfortable, the way he looked at her. "I've seen you around," Dennis said, smiling. He had one of those faces that was pleasant to look at. His eyes were nice, but Diane also knew from experience that true psychopaths had a way of looking just like that. Her ex-husband had looked like that. At just the mere thought, Diane put up her guard. On the other hand, she thought, it was good to have someone big like this Dennis-fellow close by, should it be needed. If he was as good a guy as he seemed, that was. Diane was naturally suspicious of all men.

"Welcome. Let me know if you need anything, okay?" he said. "I live right over there and can keep an eye on you from my windows. And I am quite the handyman. My wife will testify to that. You just come knocking if you need help with anything. Anything, all right?"

"Thank you," Diane said.

"No problem. Now I have to go. I'm late for work," he said and took off.

"He's a security guard," Jean said when he was gone. "Works for some big security company taking care of houses in the gated communities, you know rich folks, the ones that can afford to protect themselves. But he's good to have around. Makes us single gals feel safer."

"That's good," Diane said.

She looked at the house next door when a couple walked out, obviously fighting loudly. The sound of the man's voice talking harshly, even though he was trying to keep it down, made Diane squirm. She clenched her fist so hard it hurt where her nails dug into her skin.

"Those two are your neighbors, Tim and Tiffany. They're always at it, fighting, but both of them are nice. She'll badmouth him all day long, and he'll yell at her, but I think they love each other in their own twisted way if you know what I mean."

Diane didn't. Fighting and hurting each other had nothing to do with love. Diane had learned that much in her life.

"Now, your neighbor on the other side is a little trickier," Jean said and pointed at the house to Diane's right. "Mr. Fogerty is a little creepy if you ask me, at least most kids around here think so, but personally I don't think he'd hurt a fly. His wife died ten years ago, and he never remarried. He's only sixty-five. He could still get some gal, if you ask me, and have many years left with her, but I don't know if he's even interested. It doesn’t seem like it. He's also a dogcatcher and knows every corner of town if you ever need directions."

"How did she die?" Diane asked absent-mindedly.

"Who? His wife? Heck, I don't know. It happened before he moved here, so you'll have to ask him that yourself. But I have a feeling something bad happened. He doesn’t like to talk about it. Oh, by the way, we're having a block party in two weeks. We decorate the houses, and then the kids come to our doors and get cake or candy, while the adults get a drink, any drink you come up with. I usually make Jell-O shots, so you might want to steer clear of those. But it's fun and a chance for you to get to know everyone. Anyway, I should get going. If you need anything, I'll be right down the road."

Diane smiled. "I'll remember that. Thank you so much."

Jean gave her a look that Diane for one second thought was concern, then waved and walked on. Diane stood for a few seconds, watching her as she walked—almost swayed down the street. Diane then shook her head and turned around to walk back into the house. Misty sat in the doorway, looking up at her.

"All right, Misty. Now, we've cleaned out the living room. What's next? The kitchen? Yes, let's do the kitchen. We need to get it nice and ready so that we can cook."

Diane walked inside and looked around at how much she had accomplished so far. It was beginning to look better, but there was still a long way to go. Diane felt how tired she was, but there was no time for a break. She had to be done as soon as possible so she could start searching for jobs. She had spent all her money on the down payment for the house and didn't even have enough left to buy furniture, so she slept on an old mattress that someone had left in the living room. She had left most of her stuff back in Massachusetts when she left, and only had one box of personal belongings and two suitcases with clothes. That was all. The little she had left in her bank account after buying the house would be spent on food. She was in dire need of a job, and she knew exactly where, or at least who, to ask for help.

CHAPTER TEN

August 2018

I dropped Tyler off at the daycare center, then drove back home. I was planning on going to the station today and finishing the latest report on our investigation of the woman who had kidnapped the girls back in May. We were almost done with the case and about to close it, but I still needed to add one report from the forensics' department. It was no big deal, but I had kept postponing it, and it was all we needed to be able to close it and move on.

But as I had looked out the window of our beach house this morning, I had seen waves so big and glassy; there was no way I could ignore them.

Besides, all the kids were out of the house. I deserved some me-time.

I drove down A1A, past my parent's motel by 35th Street, and parked in my own driveway. I turned the engine off and sat there for just a second, enjoying the silence. It had been a tough couple of months, being all alone with all those children, and I couldn't remember the last time I had experienced real silence.

I closed my eyes with a deep sigh, then got out and walked inside the house. Through the sliding doors in the living room, I could see the waves crashing on the shore. They had to be at least shoulder to head-high.

Just what I needed right now. A little sea-therapy.

I rushed up the stairs and into my closet to pull out my trunks when I heard the TV blasting from the bedroom next door.

Emily.

I held the trunks between my hands, then put them down while still hearing the waves outside my window, luring me out there.

But I couldn't. Not yet.

I walked to Emily's bedroom, then knocked, taking in a deep breath. I had hardly seen her all summer and, every time I did, I found it harder and harder to talk to her. I didn't want us to fight, but that seemed to be all we did lately.

She didn't answer, so I ended up opening the door anyway. I peeked inside with a smile.

"Good morning, sweetie."

She was lying in her bed on her stomach, staring at the TV. I could see her spine through her shirt. Her bony arm was holding the remote. The sight of it made me feel sick with worry.

She didn't even look at me. I walked inside anyway. "So, what are you up to today?" I said and pulled the curtains aside to let in the sun. Emily complained and turned away from the sun.

"Jack, please stop it."

Jack. I hated—no loathed it when she called me that. I had adopted her when she was just a young child and my partner—and her mother—had been killed. I had been the only adult in her life since then. That made me her dad, and I had tried to explain to her that she should call me that. She did for some years when she was younger, but since her teenage rebellion had started, we were back to just Jack. Adopting her and becoming her parent had proved to be a lot harder than expected. We came from very different backgrounds, and there was so much I didn't understand about being black and growing up in a white home. Her mother had been born here in the States, but her grandparents had moved to Florida from the Bahamas back in the day.

"Emily," I said with a deep sigh. "Please tell me you have plans to get outside of this room today."

"Why?" she asked, still without looking up at me.

"Because you can't stay in here for the rest of your life. Dang it, Emily, you're nineteen. You should be out there in the world, having some fun, and getting on with your life."

She shrugged and continued to watch the TV. I grabbed the remote and turned it off.

"Hey!" she complained.

"Emily, you can't keep doing this. You stay in this room all day; we don't hear a word from you, you don't even come down to eat."

"If you'd let me go running, I'd be outside," she said.

"You're not going running; you're not supposed to do any exercise. The doctors at the clinic said that when they released you, remember? Not until you get your weight above ninety pounds. That was the deal. And you haven't kept that deal, have you?"

"Why would I?" she said with another shrug.

I felt like crying, just from looking at her small frame, her tiny, fragile body that seemed like it would break if I even touched her. I missed my happy sweet little Emily. I missed seeing her eating, seeing her playing and laughing happily. Where did that girl go?

Two years ago, she had fainted during Shannon's and my wedding, and we had taken her to a clinic for eating disorders in Orlando, but Emily hadn't wanted to work with them. They had kept her for three months before they finally had to give up. Now and then, I would threaten to send her back, but now that she was nineteen, I was no longer her guardian. She could make her own decisions, and so she did. I was just happy that she hadn't talked about moving away from home yet since that would be the end of her. She wouldn't be able to handle being all alone. She would just start exercising wildly again while not eating and then she would end up in the hospital shortly after. If she didn't die first.

The thought made my stomach churn. I loved that kid so much, and it tore me apart to know that she didn't want my love anymore, that I couldn't help her out of this strange state she was in. I kept waiting for it to stop, to phase out, but nothing happened. It was like life continued for everyone else, but Emily had stopped living. She simply refused to live her life.

"Did you look at the brochures I gave you?" I asked and looked at the pile of college brochures I had put on her dresser. It was obvious they hadn't been touched.

"Why would I?" she asked.

My eyes met hers, and I saw nothing but apathy. The doctors at the clinic had explained to us that her brain was sort of going in circles because of the lack of nourishment. Because she was so skinny, it was like she couldn't see any hope; she couldn't even think of the future. All she saw was her own reflection, and she didn't like it. All she saw was the fat that her mind told her she had on her body. All she could think about was wanting to lose more weight. With the weight she was maintaining right now, she was barely keeping it alive.

"Because you need to get on with your life, Emily. I told you we can pay for any college, as long as you stay close enough to live at home. I want to be able to keep an eye on you until you get better."

"So, that doesn’t really mean any college, does

it? That means a local community college," she said.

"Or UCF. And only as a start, Emily. Once you get better, we don't mind sending you to a more prestigious college, but we need to know that you will be eating once you get there, that you won't just continue to starve yourself because that will end up killing you eventually."

I spoke with a tone as soft as I could muster. In reality, I just wanted to shake her. I wanted to yell at her and get some sense into that tiny head of hers. I wanted to get her to answer my questions about why she was doing this to herself because I didn't understand. I thought I had been a great dad. I had cared greatly for her. I had loved her.

Why was she doing this to me?

"You done? I want to get back to my show," she said.

I rubbed my forehead. "I'll leave if you promise to eat breakfast."

"Sure," she said. "I'll grab something later."

I stared at her, knowing she was just placating me. We both knew she was lying. She hadn't eaten much for months, and she was heading for another hospitalization if things didn't change soon.

CHAPTER ELEVEN

I was bigger than the father, which naturally counted to my advantage. But he was strong and didn't give up without a fight. He threw himself at me, and I couldn't really get the knife in the right position. I managed to poke it against his jeans, but it didn't really go through the fabric. It was a terrible knife, one that I had bought at a thrift store thinking it would be able to do the trick. Thinking back on it, it makes me shake my head. I was so young and inexperienced.

But even without the use of the knife, I managed to fight myself up on top of the father and pin him to the floor. Holding both his arms down with my one hand and using all my weight to press him to the tiles, I punched him with my free hand. I had to punch him a lot of times and blood spurted out of his nose, but still, he was fighting me. I grabbed the knife and stabbed him in the shoulder while his wife screamed behind me. Blood gushed out of the wound, and I was overwhelmed to see it run out like that. Then I knocked him out. One last punch was all it took. I pulled out his belt from his pants and wrapped it around his neck, then tightened it as hard as I could. The wife screamed, and the man soon woke up again, only to gasp for air, his face red and bloated, the veins in his head and on his throat popping out. I remember the rush of adrenaline running through my body as he opened his eyes and stared into mine, squirming underneath me, fighting for his life. Having never killed before, this was extraordinary. It was just as I had imagined it while lying in my bed on endless nights, but even better. It was the feeling of absolute power.

Seeing her husband fight for his life made the wife stop screaming. Her screaming soon turned into an almost groaning whimper as the shock and realization of what was going on settled in her fragile body and mind. The father was still squirming beneath me, and I remember being surprised at how much strength it took to strangle a human and at how long it actually took before he died. That was when I began to contemplate what to do next. Because I wanted to stay on top of him, I wanted to see him die, look at his face and see what happened to it in the seconds when his body gave up—that was, after all, what I had fantasized about doing—but at the same time, I needed to get on with what I had started. The wife wouldn't stay where she was; she wouldn't remain in shock for long. She would go for the phone or a weapon to fight with.

As I turned my head to look at her, she backed up, whimpering, grasping for a kitchen knife. But I was faster than her. I jumped up and ran for her, then grabbed her by the wrist before she got to the knives. The look in her eyes as she looked up at me, while I held onto her arm, I will never forget. Such terror and fear, it made my heart pound.

I was amazed that she didn't scream louder than she actually did, and after thinking it over and over in my mind later, I have come to the conclusion that maybe she was in such deep shock and horror that she simply couldn't scream or even fathom what was going to happen to her. Her screams were a lot more like crying and whimpering, which suited me well in terms of the neighbors hearing us and calling for help.

I pulled her through the kitchen by the arm, then pulled out a cord from the wall, detached it from the lamp it belonged to, and used it to tie up her wrists and ankles. I grabbed a plastic bag and put it over her head and used cords to bind it with. I sat with her for a few seconds, watching her fight to breathe behind the plastic until she took her last breath, then dragged the two bodies up the stairs and placed them in the bedroom. I walked to the room next to it, where I found the two crying kids. I told them their mom and dad were sleeping and not to be afraid. They didn't believe me, naturally. Right before I put bags over their heads as well, I told them they'd be with their parents in Heaven soon. I sat with them till they stopped breathing. I held the girl's hand and stroked it gently till it was all over since she was the one who was most afraid.

I know that while reading this, you might think I am a monster, and I guess I am. But as I said, I am not the only one. If you take a closer look, you will find monsters just like me in places you would never have imagined. Most people walk around life wearing blindfolds. I dare you to take yours off and see the world for what it really is. See the evil surrounding you even in your well-trimmed suburban neighborhood.

CHAPTER TWELVE

August 2018

I went surfing. Frustrated over Emily, I threw myself into the waves as if I expected the saltwater to wash away my sadness and the overwhelming feeling of helplessness.

It didn't help.

I stayed out there for about an hour, catching one super glassy bomb after another, but having no fun at all.

So, I went to work instead.

I finished up the report on the kidnapping case and sent it off to the prosecutor, letting a sense of relief rush over me as I let go of the case. Now, I could focus solely on our new case, finding out who killed Mrs. Reynolds and her daughter and scared her son enough to run into the street. It was always with mixed emotions that I closed a case, since I worried that I hadn't been thorough enough, and it would absolutely kill me if a murderer was let go just because of a technicality.

My new case was going slowly, as I was still waiting for the two autopsy reports and the findings at the house. The boy was still alive but fighting for his life. He wasn't going to be able to help me anytime soon, even though I had a feeling he had been face to face with the killer himself. Only fifteen years old and already faced with the darkest evil in life. It was hard to think about. Almost unbearable.

On my way back from work, I stopped at my parents' motel. As usual, the kids would be dropped off by the bus right outside their motel, and they'd stay there till I was off work. Usually, we would end up eating together, and tonight, my parents had even promised to throw a couple of fish on the grill. A little back-to-school celebration. My dad loved to go fishing in the mornings, and I hoped he had caught some good ones. It was grouper season, and those were my favorite.

I parked the Jeep outside in the parking lot and noticed that it was almost empty. I liked when the place grew quiet once summer was over. It was selfish because, of course, I wanted my parents to have a lot of business and make a living, but I absolutely loved when the motel was almost empty, and I could have my parents to myself. Just the kids and us. Just our family.

"Hi there, son," my dad yelled. He was coming out of the door to one of the rooms, holding his toolbox in his hand.

"Hi, Dad. Another clogged drain?" I asked.

"Nah, just fixed a chair. A leg had fallen off, but it hadn't broken. How about you? Had a good day?" He nodded toward the ocean where the waves were still crashing. "Did you get some this morning?"

"Sure did," I said. "Before work."

My dad laughed and patted my shoulder. "I'm guessing someone is happy to have the kids back in school, huh?"

I breathed in the fresh salty air, then exhaled. "I would be lying if I said no," I said with a chuckle.

"It's understandable you'd feel that way," my dad said. "You deserve a break. All those kids. Phew. I don't know how you do it."

"I'll let you in on a little secret there, Dad. Neither do I."

He laughed again and patted my shoulder. "I'll

just put these tools away. Your mom is inside with Tyler. She picked him up a little early to spend some time with him on the beach before the older kids got back. I hope you don't mind."

"Are you kidding me? No, that's wonderful," I said, relieved. I had felt guilty leaving Tyler at the day care all day since he wasn't really used to being away that much yet.

"Good, good. Now, I have to go wash up before dinner. Caught a couple of gorgeous groupers this morning. Can't wait to show you."

"And I can't wait to eat them," I said, hearing my stomach rumble. As I watched my dad walk up the stairs to the private quarters above the motel, I couldn't help feeling so grateful for having my parents here to help me while Shannon was away. They truly were a blessing in my life.

CHAPTER THIRTEEN

August 2018

I found my mom inside the motel's kitchen, standing at the stove, tasting something.

"Hi, Mom," I said.

"Jack! Come here and taste this sauce; tell me what's missing."

I approached her and tasted it. "A little more thyme," I said. "Then it's perfect."

My mom grinned, then winked at me. "I knew I could count on my son to help me out."

"Where is Tyler?" I asked and looked around.

My mom turned around and pointed. Through the door came a woman, holding Tyler by the hand.

"Daddy-y-y-y-y!" Tyler yelled and ran to me. I

picked him up and kissed him gently on the forehead.

"Hi there, buddy. How was your day?"

"'Nita."

"'Nita? What's that supposed to mean?" I asked, puzzled.

"He keeps saying that. We think it's a girl," my mom said and threw the thyme in the sauce as I had suggested. "Her name could be Anita or something close to that. We think he met her at the day care center, but we're not completely sure about that yet. Further investigation is needed."

My mom turned her head and winked at Tyler. I stared at the woman by the door. She smiled and, as her eyes met mine, I knew right away that they were familiar but, at first, I couldn't place them. Then it hit me.

"Diane?"

"Yes," my mom said. "Is it wonderful? Diane moved here just recently."

"I…I can't believe it," I said. "Is it really you? I haven't seen you since…well, how long has it been?"

"Since senior year," she said.

"Almost twenty years," my mom said.

"No. It can't be," I argued. "I'm not that old, am I? Twenty years since we graduated?"

"I am afraid she's right," Diane said.

"So…what brings you here?" I asked. "You moved here?"

She nodded. "About a week ago."

"She bought a house up on Suwannee Lane," my mom said and added salt to her sauce as well.

"Really?" I asked.

Diane nodded. "Close to the ocean and everything. It's small and needs a lot of fixing up, but I think I can make a home of it…eventually."

"Wow," I said. "That's…that's wonderful."

"Isn't it?" My mom said and grabbed the pot with the sauce between her hands. She smiled from ear to ear as she looked at Diane. I knew she had always been fond of her back in the day. I guess I was quite excited to see her too.

"She came here to ask for a job, so I invited her to stay for dinner," my mom said.

"A job?" I said. "Here at the motel?"

I felt a pinch of worry in the pit of my stomach. I knew my parents were struggling a little financially to make ends meet, but I also knew they could never say no to someone like Diane if she came asking for a job. But could they afford to have one more on the payroll?

"I know what you're thinking," my mom said, giving me one of her looks that usually meant I should stay out of it. "But I'm not getting any younger, and I could use an extra hand or two around here. We'll make it work, won't we, Diane?"

Diane smiled and nodded. "I sure hope so."

"Then that's a deal," my mom said. "You start tomorrow. Now, let's gather the kids; it's time to eat."

As I walked out the door, my mom stopped me. She leaned over and said in a low voice:

"Emily's not coming tonight either?"

I sighed and shook my head. "I'm afraid not."

CHAPTER FOURTEEN

August 2018

She called him during intermission. It wasn't something she usually did, calling Jack in the middle of her concert since she was usually so preoccupied with her show and focused on doing it perfectly, but tonight, she needed to hear his voice. The pain in her hand was too unbearable, and she needed to talk to the man she loved.

Shannon rushed to her dressing room, found her phone, then cursed because her hand pained her so deeply before she found his number.

"Hi, babe," Jack said.

His voice sounded cheerful. In the background, she could hear the voices of all the children. The sound filled her with such deep longing it was almost unbearable.

"Shannon? What's up? I thought you had a concert."

"I do," she said pressing back tears. "I…I just missed you so much and wanted to say hi to you."

"We've just finished eating the most amazing grouper that my dad caught this morning," he said.

Shannon could hear the twins arguing in the background and realized she even missed that.

What am I doing so far away from home?

"Did the concert go all right?" Jack asked. "Did something happen? Are you okay?"

She sniffled and swallowed. "Yeah, yeah, I'm fine. I just…really missed you that's all."

"I miss you too. You have no idea. And the kids too. Here, you can say hello to them real quick."

Shannon heard the phone moving and Jack yelled in the distance.

"Everyone! Hey, kids. Angela, Austin, Abigail, Betsy Sue, everyone, say hello to Shannon."

She could hear all of their little voices as they yelled hello Shannon and hello mommy to her and then she heard Tyler almost scream her name out. It made her heart drop.

"There you go," Jack said as he returned on the phone. "They all miss you."

"I miss them too. Terribly."

"Oh, and gucss what? Someone else is here," he said.

"Who's that?" she said, wiping a tear off her cheek that refused to be held back.

"Diane."

"Who is Diane?" Shannon asked, a little confused.

"I told you about Diane, didn't I?" Jack said.

"I don't know, Jack…I don't remember…oh… you mean as in your high school sweetheart, Diane?" Shannon said, suddenly sitting up straight on her couch. The smell from the fresh flowers in front of her was a little too overwhelming and gave her nausea. Maybe it wasn't the flowers.

"Yes, that's her. You won't believe it. She just moved to Cocoa Beach. Isn't that funny?"

"I'm laughing already," she said. "And she's with you…right now? At your parents' motel, eating with…our kids?"

Sitting in my chair?

"Yes," he said. "She came here looking for work, and my mom hired her. Then, she invited her to stay for dinner. They used to be close, back in the day. She had a troubled childhood and my parents' home was a safe haven for her."

"You don't say."

Shannon swallowed hard, and then there was a knock on her door. "Mrs. King? It's time."

"Be right there," she yelled back, then returned to the phone. "Listen, Jack. I gotta go. Kiss the kids from me, will you? Especially Tyler."

"Of course. Now knock them out of the park, will you? I know you'll be fabulous," Jack said.

Shannon hung up and let the tears roll across her cheeks. As she wiped them off and corrected her make-up, she couldn't stop imagining this girl, this old flame of Jack's sitting at the table with her family. As she walked out and put on her stage smile, she couldn't help thinking that she wasn't going to be that hard to replace.

CHAPTER FIFTEEN

Cocoa Beach 2007

"Happy birthday to yo-o-u, happy birthday to y-ou-u-u."

The boy felt his heart skip a beat as the cupcake was brought in with the one little candle in it, as was the custom on the boy's birthday. They couldn't really afford a real cake—except when baby sister turned one year old, but that was an exceptional birthday his dad had told him since it was her first —so, usually, his dad would buy him a cupcake on his way home from work and serve it to him after dinner. As his dad sang to him, his mom stared at him, her arms crossed across her chest, an annoyed look on her face.

The cupcake landed on the table in front of the boy, and he gleamed as he looked up at his father.

"Happy birthday, son."

"Thanks, Dad," he said.

His mom made a smacking sound with her lips, and the boy turned to look at her, looking for any sign that she too was happy it was his birthday, that she also wanted to wish him a happy birthday.

But he saw none of that. Since she was probably just exhausted from taking care of the baby, the boy excused her. The same way his dad always did.

That baby is going to end up wearing Mom out.

"I have a present for you," his dad said.

His mom let out a deep exhale the same way she had done on the night before when Dad had cooked for her, and she didn't like it. Again, Dad had told him that Mommy couldn't help herself. She was so tired all the time, and he had put a little too much salt on the potatoes, he had to admit.

The boy hadn't thought there was too much salt in any of the delicious food his dad had prepared. He had thought it tasted heavenly. But, of course, what did a young boy like him know?

Not much, according to his momma. According to her, boys didn't understand much of anything, and they certainly weren't as pretty and cute as little girls. The boy had learned that much.

"What is it, Daddy?" the boy said, shrieking in excitement. Last year, the boy hadn't gotten any presents for his birthday, since Mommy had said they couldn't afford it, with just having given birth to the baby and all, and with all the things they needed to buy for her, like stuffed animals and such. Things the boy had never gotten, but then again, she was a girl and girls were cuter and prettier and smelled better than boys. That's what Momma said.

"Come with me, son," his dad said and reached out his hand.

"So, you're just gonna leave like that? With the kitchen a mess?" his mom said while sitting with his baby sister on her lap, making funny noises at her and making her giggle.

The boy ignored his mother's remark because his dad did, then rushed out after him into the yard.

"I asked you something," Momma yelled after them but, for once, what she said wasn't the most important thing in the world, the boy realized. His dad had something that was way more exciting.

"Close your eyes," his dad said as they walked into the yard.

The boy was overwhelmed with excitement as

he let his dad guide him through the tall grass that the dad should have cut many weeks ago but hadn't had the time to because of all the other stuff that needed to be done to the house to make Mommy's life easier.

"What is it, Dad? Tell me what it is?" the boy said, almost about to explode with happiness and anticipation. The boy had never had a surprise before. Never. Except for the time they had told him he was going to be a big brother. That had been a surprise all right.

"Just one more second," his dad said and pulled him further, then stopped. "Now, open your eyes."

The boy took in a breath of air, braced himself for a big surprise, then opened his eyes. He looked at the fence in front of him, then up at his dad, his eyes and mouth wide open.

"Chickens?"

His dad smiled and laughed. "Yes, son. Two chickens. Isabella and Victoria. I named them. If you don't like the names, then you can call them something else. But they're yours now, son."

The boy stared at the two chickens inside the enclosure that his dad had built for them. He couldn't believe his own eyes. The boy absolutely loved animals, and chickens were among his favorites.

"Between us, I wanted to give you a puppy, but your mom wouldn't hear of it. Chickens, I could get her to agree to since they stay outside. Look at them. Aren't they cute?"

The boy looked at the two chickens and then decided that his dad was wrong. They weren't cute because that's what his sister was, and these two creatures were nothing like his baby sister. No, these chickens were a lot more than that. They were what he needed in his life right now. They were amazing.

CHAPTER SIXTEEN

August 2018

She was scrubbing the kitchen floor, getting layers of dirt off, when she saw the stain. At first, she thought it was just dirt, but the more she scrubbed, the more Diane realized it wasn't just ordinary dirt on the planks of her newly bought house.

It was blood.

Diane stared at the stain, then at her hands where the red had rubbed off and become mixed with the soapy water, turning it almost pink. Diane looked down at the planks again. She had been scrubbing for quite some time on the stain, yet there seemed to be a lot more. The blood had to have seeped deep inside the planks. And there was a lot of it.

Diane rose to her knees with an odd sensation in her stomach. Trying to calm herself down, she got up to her feet and walked a few steps back, her heart beginning to pound in her chest. Misty came closer and was about to walk into the mess when Diana stopped the cat and picked it up. She thought about going across the street and asking Dennis to come to take a look at it, but she knew he had a family and she didn't know him that well. Maybe Jean? Diane shook her head; no, she wouldn't know what to do. Diane walked to the counter and grabbed her phone and called Jack. He was a detective. He would know what to do. After they had finished dinner tonight, and she had told him that he and his parents were the only people she knew in this town, he had given her his number and told her to call him if she needed anything. Anything at all.

"Ryder here," he said as he picked up. He sounded tired.

"It's Diane."

She could hear a child crying in the background and looked at her watch. It was past eleven.

Oh, crap. It's that late?

"Sorry, did I wake anyone up?" she asked. "I'm

so sorry."

"Oh, no. It's just Tyler. He doesn't want to go to sleep. He does this every night. There's nothing new in that. He was already awake when you called. What's up?"

"I was cleaning my new house and then…well, I found a big stain of blood on the kitchen floor. I don't know what to do…"

"Uh-huh. Okay. Something might have happened in there while it was empty. Or maybe a homeless person slept there and hurt himself. Try not to touch anything, and I'll come look at it tomorrow," he said. "It might be nothing."

Diane swallowed and looked at the area. It had been covered in dirt and dust, so that was why she hadn't noticed earlier.

"Okay," she said. "I hope you're right."

"All right. I should get this kid to bed. He seems to be tired enough now. See you tomorrow," Jack said.

"Yes, okay."

She put the phone back on the counter with a deep uneasy sensation in the pit of her stomach. She petted the cat while staring at the blood stain. Then she grabbed her pillow and a blanket and walked out onto the porch.

CHAPTER SEVENTEEN

August 2018

I skipped surfing the next morning and drove to Diane's house instead. We had a meeting about the Reynolds case at noon, so that left me with plenty of time to take a look at the stain in Diane's house. I knew it was probably a huge waste of my time. It was probably nothing, and usually, I would just tell her not to get worked up about it, but she had sounded so nervous and worried on the phone, I thought it'd be best if I showed up in person.

There was something different about Diane. She wasn't quite the happy and confident girl I had dated back then. She seemed shaken and anxious, and that was very different from what she had been back in high school. I felt like she needed my protection.

I parked in her driveway and walked up to the small house. It was cute—or at least it had been once—but the entire lot and parts of the house were completely overgrown, and the wood needed a serious paint job.

I found Diane on the porch, sitting on an old mattress with a cat in her lap.

"Diane?' I asked.

She looked up. Her eyes were red. I stared at her pillow and blanket. "Did you sleep out here?"

She nodded.

"That must have been terribly hot," I said, sweating just from thinking about it. At this time of year, the AC at our house ran at its highest. It was also this time of year that our electric bill was through the roof.

"I…I couldn't stand sleeping inside with that… with all the…well, see for yourself," she said.

Diane rose to her feet and walked to the door. I couldn't believe that she didn't want to stay inside just because of a little blood on the floor. Why didn't she just choose another room?

"It's right over here," she said and walked me

into the kitchen. The planks had dried-up soap on top, but I could easily see the blood on them.

"It's all this area, and then it continues over here and to the stairs, and on each and every step," she said and pointed. "Look. It's like someone who was bleeding was dragged up the stairs." Diane shot me an anxious look. "Who was bleeding this much, Jack? Who?"

I sighed and squatted to better look at it. There were several layers of thick dirt on top of it, but as I looked closer, I could see the blood underneath. "It looks old," I said. "Maybe it was the last owner? Maybe whoever lived here had an accident or something?"

"What kind of accident?" Diane asked nervously.

"I...I don't know. But I wouldn't worry about it."

"So, you think I can just wash it off then? You don't need to investigate it?"

"I hardly think so," I said. "Besides, we're pretty swamped lately. If there's no one hurt, or signs of any crime committed, I think we'll be fine."

"But what if there was?" she said. "The thing is, I really want to remove the planks and put in tile instead."

"Diane, I'm sure it'll be fine. The house is yours. Do with it what you need to, okay?"

My phone was vibrating in my pocket. I pulled it out. It was Shannon. I decided to call her back after my visit here. As I put the phone back, I realized I was standing in a completely empty house.

"Say…where's your furniture?" I asked.

"I…I don't have any. At least not yet. With my job at your parent's place, I hope to be able to buy some. Eventually."

"But…but that's gonna take forever. You don't even have a bed?" I asked, baffled. "You can't live like this, Diane."

She sighed. "I'll be fine. It's better than where I came from; believe me. Way better."

CHAPTER EIGHTEEN

After my first kill, I got paranoid. It was probably only natural, and I'm assuming all killers go through a phase like that right after they've acted their fantasies out for the first time. But it was a tough time for me. I was constantly terrified they were going to come for me. I was certain they would. I even began expecting them to. Every day, I waited for them to come; every day, I imagined them knocking on my door. I imagined them driving up the street, and every time a car did pass the house, I jumped, wondering if that could be them.

Sometimes, I imagined they only arrived in two cars; other times, there were ten. How many officers were there changed from time to time, also how aggressively they entered the house. Sometimes, they knocked nicely and asked me calmly to come with them; other times, they came from all sides, guns blazing, yelling and screaming at me to get down. I even had little conversations in my mind with them. I knew what they were going to say, what questions they would ask me, and I had prepared all the answers. I knew exactly what I was going to tell them.

I wasn't going to lie. I would admit to each and every detail of it. I mean, why not? They knew I had done it and, to be frank, I was proud of it. I wasn't going to try and wiggle my way out of it. There was no need to. I hadn't prepared an excuse for what I had done either. I wasn't even going to try to. I knew it was the evil inside of me. It was the rage that had finally been allowed to surface and demanded that I do it. There was no excuse. Was I sorry? Not really, no. Did I feel bad for what I had done? Not really, no. I knew something was wrong with me and I knew that was why I had these thoughts, why I constantly fantasized about killing to a point where I had to do it, where I couldn't ignore it anymore.

The only thing I really felt, to be honest, was a desire to do it again. It's sad, I know. But it's the truth. The naked truth.

As the days passed and the police didn't come, I started to think that maybe, just maybe I was actually going to get away with it. I watched them as they talked to the neighbors, as they questioned the nice couple across the street, and I even watched one of the men from further down the road being hauled off in a police car, and people started to talk about him being a suspect and maybe having killed more than just the poor family. Some even used the words serial killer.

I liked the sound of that.

I listened to them talk; I heard them say those things with a slight quiver to their voices, and that was when I realized that I wanted that. I wanted them to fear me. I wanted them to talk about me like that. I liked the sensation of them fearing me, of them shivering from talking about me, and meanwhile, I was standing right there, right next to them, living and being in their midst. That was what had me going. That was what I wanted more of.

I wanted people to be scared of me.

So, as time passed and no one even remotely looked my way or asked me any questions that showed they thought I might be the killer, I began a new phase in my life.

I started to plan my next move.

CHAPTER NINETEEN

August 2018

"Where are we on the Reynolds' case, Jack?"

Weasel stood in the corner of the meeting room, pouring herself coffee from the pot. Her real name was Weslie Seal, but only a few knew that since she had been nothing but the Weasel since high school. She had put her dyed blond hair in a ponytail and was wearing a leather jacket over her broad shoulders. Her raspy, hoarse voice cut through me, mostly because I didn't really have an answer prepared.

"Well, so far, we don't really know much," I said and opened the file. "From the forensics report, we know that the mother was probably attacked in the kitchen, and the killer probably entered through the back door. She was then dragged into the living room, where the killer tied her up using cords that he cut off from the lamps in there. She was tied on both wrists and ankles. Now, the medical examiner says that she was alive when the killer began the separation of the head from the neck. It was done with an ax that was later found in the garage. Other than the chopping off of her head, her body was only lightly bruised, so we assume she cooperated with the killer, probably thinking he would eventually let her go if she did as he told her to, or at least spare the children. This is all just speculation, of course. But what we do know for certain is that she died there on the floor sometime between six-fifty when her alarm clock went off and eight o'clock, according to the autopsy. We know that she would have left before eight o'clock since she had to be at work at the jewelry store in Cape Canaveral at eight. It's a drive that takes seven minutes from the house where they live. The daughter, however, was probably surprised in her bedroom when the killer rushed in there after killing the mother. The music was still playing loudly from her computer when the police arrived, so we assume she hadn't heard anything while she was getting ready for school that starts at eight. She too was killed between six-fifty and eight o'clock; that is the closest we can get to an exact time of her death. A clear plastic bag was placed on her head first before she was tied up. The cause of death was strangulation. The young girl had more bruises on her body and her face. We believe she fought more intensely than her mother. We have conducted interviews with the neighbors and friends of the family, and I have asked the husband to come in again later today for a second interview. The two of them were separated but not divorced, even though it was years since they split up. According to friends, the husband didn't want to give her the divorce. There was also an ongoing dispute about the children."

Weasel nodded. "Okay, and what has he told you so far?"

I looked at Mike, sitting further down from me. "Mike was the one who spoke to him initially."

"All right, Mike?" she said and sipped her coffee.

"There really wasn't much he could tell us; he was quite shocked," Mike said. "Which is quite understandable when he just lost his wife—even though she was an ex—and his kid and he might lose the second child as well."

"When was the last time he saw them?"

"He wasn't in the picture much," Mike said. "He said she kept the kids away from him, but the last time he saw them was at spring break when Parker and Olivia came down to visit for two days."

"He hadn't seen them since spring break?" Weasel said.

"Nope. He said his ex always came up with excuses for the kids not to visit. And as time passed by, he simply stopped fighting her and took what he could get."

"Kind of gives him a motive," Joe Hall said. He was one of the younger officers at the station.

"True," I said. "But why kill the daughter too?"

"Affect," Weasel said. "Rage. He was angry with all of them. Blamed them for his loneliness. Or maybe the girl surprised him and then he had to kill her too not to get caught."

"In my opinion, the killings didn't exactly look like they were done in affect," I said. "They seemed calculated. Planned out. Using the bags and tying them up and everything. It wasn't a sudden thing. He didn't accidentally kill them."

"Jack's got a point," Joe Hall said.

"He does," Weasel said. "But let's grill the dad

some more before we decide who's right, okay? Give him all you've got this afternoon."

"Will do," I said.

"Did he have an alibi?" Weasel added.

Mike Wagner shook his head. "Not a bullet-proof one. They were killed in the morning, right before they were about to leave for school and work. At that time, Jim—that's the dad—was getting ready for work himself. He works as a security guard for KDL."

"Check the GPS in his phone for his where-abouts on that morning," Weasel said.

"He could have left the phone at home," I argued.

"Still, if it places him at the scene, then we have something to go by," Weasel said. "Now the boy, Parker. What do we know about him?"

"He's still fighting for his life," I said. "I spoke to the hospital this morning, and there has been no improvement. We know that he goes to Cocoa Beach Jr./Sr. High, where he just started tenth grade. The teachers there love him, and all say he's a great kid. They don't know of any family prob-lems at home or with the dad."

"All right," she said. "Did he suffer any abuse before he ran into the street?"

I shook my head. "It's hard to tell, but the doctors don't think so. He might have seen what happened and then just run away."

"So, no bruises on wrists or arms where the killer might have tried to hold him?" Weasel asked.

"Not according to the doctors, no," I said. "My guess is the killer never got to him."

"Okay, so maybe the killer doesn't know that he saw what happened, if we assume he did."

"That was my next point," I said. "I think we need to put a guard up at the hospital in case the killer finds out he survived. He might want to get rid of him."

Weasel nodded. "Good thinking. I'll have that done right away. All right, people. We need to get back to work. I need a volunteer to attend "Coffee with the Mayor" tonight. You know, just to make sure no crazy person decides to attack him because of the red tide in the rivers or anything. Moods around here are quite agitated lately."

"I'll do it," Marty said. He had been very quiet through it all, and that was unusual for Marty during briefings. He was usually a jokester and a funny guy, but I guess this case had taken its toll on him as well. I couldn't blame him. He was an excellent choice for the "Coffee with the Mayor" event.

It was usually a very nice event where the citizens of Cocoa Beach could come and ask the mayor about anything concerning the town, but lately, the meetings had become quite agitated due to the dirty water in our canals and rivers. I couldn't blame people for being angry, but I wasn't sure our poor Mayor Campbell could do much about it. This was an issue all over Florida, not just Cocoa Beach.

The door opened, and someone poked her head in. It was Cassandra, the new face at the front desk.

"Detective Ryder, Mr. Reynolds is here for you."

I looked at my watch. "He's early. I'll be there in one sec."

I rose to my feet, looked at Joe hall, then asked him to come with me. It wasn't until I walked out the door that I remembered I had forgotten to call Shannon back. I decided it had to wait.

CHAPTER TWENTY

Cocoa Beach 2008

The chickens brought the boy great joy for a very long time. Even more so when they grew up, and he realized Isabella was a boy chicken and the boy renamed him Hector. Soon, Victoria started producing eggs, and the boy would give them to his momma with the result that she would smile at him. There really was nothing like making Momma smile.

Every morning, the boy ran outside and gathered the eggs from the enclosure, then rushed back to his momma and handed them to her, waiting for that particular smile and the recognition in the shape of a *Thank you* from her lips. Those two words would seem small to many, but to the boy, they meant the world because they were so rare. Even her looking at him, seeing him was so rare it would leave him exhilarated once he received it. And he did that every morning, at least for a little while.

Until one morning when baby sister suddenly decided to let go of the table and begin to walk on her own. The boy was standing in the kitchen, holding the eggs out to Mother when it happened. Mother's face changed, and suddenly she didn't look at the boy anymore. She rose to her feet with a gasp and walked to the baby, who was staggering across the floor all by herself. Now, the boy knew this was a big development since Momma had been very worried about baby sister and why she hadn't started to walk or talk yet, given she would soon turn two years old, and the boy had heard Momma and Daddy talk about it very loudly in the kitchen when they thought the boy was asleep. So, the boy understood that this was a great moment for baby sister, and he accepted the fact that Momma wasn't going to give him a smile and a Thank you, on this particular morning, and he went on about his day not worrying about it anymore. Not until the next morning when he went to gather the eggs and rushed to Momma in the kitchen only to find that she wasn't there. He heard a noise from the living room, then rushed in there and found baby sister staggering around, her arms stretched in the air, while Momma was sitting on the floor, clapping her hands at every move the child made. She didn't look at him when he entered.

"Momma?" he said.

She didn't react. The boy held out the eggs. They were still warm between his hands.

"I have your eggs?"

But his mother didn't even turn to look. Instead, she laughed and clapped as baby sister took a series of steps across the tiles with a joyful shriek, then tumbled and fell flat on her face.

"Momma?" the boy said as she rushed to the baby who let out an ear-piercing scream. "I have your eggs. Aren't you gonna take them, Momma? Please? Momma? MOMMA?"

The boy didn't even realize he had yelled it out, nor did he notice that one of the eggs had rolled out of his hand and onto the floor where it had smashed onto the carpet.

"Not now, boy," she hissed at him. "Can't you see that your sister needs me?" She grabbed baby sister into her arms and comforted her, then approached him. She didn't even look at him but spotted the smashed egg in the carpet with a deep exhale. It was followed by a quick yet painful slap across the boy's face.

"Now, look what you've done! As if I haven't enough to do around here as it is."

His mother left the living room, and as the boy stood there—his cheek burning from the slap—staring at the yellow yolk in the carpet, he clenched his fist around the other egg so hard it splattered inside of his palm and dripped onto the carpet.

He never brought his mother eggs again.

CHAPTER TWENTY-ONE

August 2018

"How many times do I have to say the same thing over and over again?"

Jim Reynolds looked at me, annoyed. He was a big man, especially when he stood up. Not only was he tall, around six feet seven or eight would be my guess. He was also very muscular, which I guessed served him well working as a security guard.

"I was getting ready for work. I had to be at my post at nine, and I was. Just ask my boss."

"We did, and he confirmed," I said.

"So, why am I here? This was my family that was attacked. I'm the one who lost someone."

"You were at your post at nine o'clock, but that

still gives you plenty of time to drive to Cocoa Beach and back," Joe Hall said.

"You clearly don't know much about morning traffic then," Jim said. "It takes at least forty-five minutes to get from Palm Bay to Cocoa Beach."

"You could have spent the night in Cocoa Beach," I said. "Or maybe driven very early, surprised them, and waited in their house till they woke up."

He leaned back in his chair with a deep sigh.

"Whatever."

I realized I was thirsty, so I drank some water from my cup. Jim hadn't touched his coffee that I had served him when he got there, trying to break the ice. It hadn't worked. The guy had all his defenses up from the beginning of the interview. It made it a lot harder to get anything out of him that we could use.

"The thing is, Jim. You have a motive. You were angry at your ex, at Amber for keeping the kids from you, am I right?"

"Who wouldn't be?" he said. "She wouldn't let me see them. I miss them, you know? But she didn't give me a chance."

"Ever think about hurting her?" I asked.

He answered with a *tsk* and an eye roll, reminding me of Emily. Everything about his behavior struck me as being a little childish.

Joe rustled some papers, then said:

"Amber applied to have a restraining order put on you three months ago. Care to explain that? She told the officer, and I quote, that 'she was afraid of you and you had hit her on several occasions.' Now, the request was denied by the court since she had no proof of the abuse, no pictures or current bruises, and she had never contacted the police for assistance, but it does paint quite the picture, doesn't it?"

Jim shook his head. "I didn't kill her, though."

"You only beat her?" I asked, repulsed. I hated wife-beaters more than anything.

"As I said, I didn't kill her. If you want to ask me more questions, I think I'll need to have a lawyer present."

I looked at Joe, then back at Jim. "I think we're done here for now anyway."

I closed the file shut. "But stay around. We might need to have another chat with you again later."

Jim leaned forward in his seat.

"I wouldn't even think about leaving. Parker is in the hospital fighting for his life. I'm all he has left. What kind of a man do you take me for?"

CHAPTER TWENTY-TWO

August 2018

I picked up Tyler from the church's daycare and brought him with me to the hospital. I had been visiting Parker every day since the accident, just to remind me why it was important that this case was solved. I was doing this for him, for his sake. If he ever woke up, I wanted to be here to tell him that we had managed to get justice for his family. The murders of his mother and sister were so brutal that I needed to catch this monster to be able to believe in the good of this world again. I had rarely faced such an evil crime scene, such evil in every way the murderer had acted toward this family. And I couldn't let evil win. Not if I was to believe that I was raising my kids into a better world. I wanted my kids to grow up knowing that justice prevailed, that evil never won.

I entered Parker Reynolds' room and left Tyler with the officer that Weasel had placed outside the room. His name was Chris and had been transferred to the Cocoa Beach department two years ago. He knew Tyler well, and the two of them had a chat while I went to look at Parker.

I pulled up a chair next to him and sat down. Parker didn't make a noise; all that told me he was still alive was the machine breathing for him. The tubes and the beeping monitors made the entire scene so incredibly creepy.

"Spoke to your dad today," I said. "I wouldn't say he was a nice guy, but then again, these types of interviews and situations tend to bring out the worst in people. I'll give him the benefit of the doubt, I guess. As of now, he's my only suspect, but I'm not sure I believe he killed your mom and your sister. I do, however, think she had her reasons for kicking him out, and I am terribly sorry that he is your only family left once you get out of here. And you will get out of here, Parker. You hear me? You'll beat this. And once you do, I will have caught this bastard. Mark my words."

I sighed and looked out the window at the river.

This had to be the hospital with the best views in the world. It was placed with river water on three sides of it, and if you were in one of the top floors like Parker was since I had pulled some strings with a few contacts I had in the hospital—you could actually see the ocean too. It was just so sad that Parker wouldn't be able to enjoy it.

I could hear Tyler squealing in the hall outside and looked at my watch. It was getting late, and my mom had dinner ready for us. It was Friday, and I was looking forward to a much-needed weekend ahead. All I wanted was to hang out on the beach with my kiddos and maybe go surfing if there were still waves. But as I said goodbye to Parker and returned to Officer Chris, I saw him hold a hand to Tyler's forehead, and I knew those plans were already spoiled.

"I think he might have a fever," Chris said.

I sighed deeply. "Oh, how great."

I grabbed Tyler in my arms and felt him myself. Yup. That was a fever all right.

I said goodbye to Chris, then returned to my car and drove to my parents' place, where I put Tyler in front of the TV and served him some mashed potatoes that he didn't eat. I watched TV with him for a few minutes till he fell asleep and I walked outside to be with my parents and all the other kids for a little while.

"Still no Emily?" my mom asked as she served me some fried chicken and mashed potatoes.

I shook my head and grabbed the beer my dad handed me. The kids all threw themselves at the food.

"I haven't seen her since yesterday. And that was just briefly when I got back from work. She hardly wants to speak to me. She stays in that room all night and all day. And she's not eating anything. When I ask her if she is, she says she ate something earlier, but I don't believe her."

My mom sat down across from me, grabbed my hand in hers, and forced me to look her in the eyes, the way she used to when I was a child, and she had something important to discuss.

"Jack. You need to do something about her. Soon."

"Don't give me that look, Mom. I'm trying my best here. What do you want me to do, huh? I've tried everything. Nothing is working."

My mom bit her lip, then said:

"Spend time with her."

"What do you mean spend time with her? I spend plenty of time with her, or I used to, but now she doesn't even want to talk to me. She'll hardly even look at me when I come into her room."

"What does every teenager ask themselves?" my mom said. "What's the one thing they ask themselves constantly?"

I sighed and shrugged, then sipped my beer. "How am I supposed to know? Who knows how teenagers think?"

"Am I loved?" my mom said. "That's what they want to know. That's what they are constantly searching for confirmation of. Children do that too, but it becomes especially pressing once they reach their teens. Does anyone love me? That's what they want to know. You need to let her feel that. You need to make her feel valuable. Like she matters to you."

I leaned back in my patio chair and sipped my beer again. "But she knows that. Doesn't she?"

"I'm not sure she does. You're not her birth father. You took her in because her mother was killed. When it was just her, then yes, I think she might have felt like she belonged, but since then, Emily has been putting herself aside for years while the twins were more important, while Tyler was. Even while Shannon and Betsy Sue became more important to you. It's her turn now. The girl has no idea who she is. You need to help her. You're her dad. You want to be her dad, right?"

"Of course. It hurts me like crazy when she calls me Jack and not dad," I said. "I hate when she does it."

"You don't become a dad just because someone calls you one, just as little as sitting in a garage makes you a car. It's time you act like one too. It's time you attend to her needs. As a dad, you know exactly what they are."

"She needs to eat, and I'm always trying to feed her," I said. "But I can't force her."

"I think it goes a little deeper than that, and I'm certain you know it does," my mom said and got up from her seat.

I watched her walk to the kitchen and bring back a key lime pie, much to the children's joy. I studied them as they threw themselves at it while wondering how my mother had become so smart. I did know exactly what Emily needed, and I had been putting it off for way too long.

CHAPTER TWENTY-THREE

August 2018

I woke up the next morning realizing I had once again forgotten to call Shannon. Actually, it wasn't until after I had served breakfast for all the kids and put Tyler down for a nap that I remembered. Tyler had been awake—and kept me awake—for most of the night, crying his little heart out. Once I saw him close his eyes and I snuck out, that was when it struck me. I was supposed to have called her back. There had just been so much.

I looked at my watch, then Angela came toward me, crying. Immediately, I forgot my phone when I saw the scrape on her knee.

"We were skateboarding outside on the pavement," she said, sobbing.

"And then you fell," I said. "It happens. Come let me clean it up for you."

We walked downstairs, and I found the first aid kit when the door slammed open, and Abigail came rushing inside, an angry look on her face.

"Austin is an idiot," she said.

"What have I told you about calling your brother names?" I asked.

She looked up at me with her big blue eyes. She was going to be such a knockout once she reached those teenage years; I had already started to dread it.

"To not to?" she said.

Carefully, I cleansed Angela's wound, while she sniffed and wiped away tears. She moved her leg in pain.

"Sit still, please," I said.

"It's all his fault, you know," Abigail said and stared at Angela's wound with huge eyes.

"This is Austin's fault?" I asked.

Abigail nodded. "He didn't want to hold Angela's hand."

"They were holding hands while on the skate-board?" I asked.

"No, because Austin didn't want to," Abigail said. "Keep up, Dad."

"If Austin doesn't want to hold someone's hand, then he doesn't have to," I said. "That doesn't mean it was his fault Angela crashed."

"Ycs, it was," Abigail said. I was getting tired of this conversation. Abigail always wanted to argue everything, and it was tiring.

I put on a Band-Aid and then looked at Angela. "There. Almost as good as new. Now, no more skateboarding, all right? Why don't you go down to the beach and play some ball or maybe go swimming, huh?"

"I wanna go surfing," Abigail said.

"That's a great idea," I said.

Abigail looked disappointed. "But no one wants to go with me." Her eyes lit up as she looked at me.

"Could you come with me; could you, Daddy, please?"

I sighed and helped Angela down from the counter. She walked back outside to be with Austin, whom she'd had a crush on since I met Shannon and she brought the girl into our lives. I didn't really know the rules for stepsiblings falling in love, but since they were only nine, I guessed we could let it go for a little while. If it still persisted when they were teenagers, then maybe we'd have to deal with it differently.

"I can't, honey. Tyler is sick, and I have to keep an eye on him. His fever is higher today than yesterday, and I need to take him to the doctor if it doesn't go down soon."

Abigail sighed. "Stupid Tyler. It's always about him. Why don't you ever spend any time with me anymore, huh? Me and Austin, we need you too!"

And with those words, she rushed out of the house and slammed the door behind her. I looked after her, shaking my head, thinking it didn't really matter how hard I tried. It was never going to be good enough, was it? Everyone wanted me to do better.

As I finished the thought, I heard Tyler cry from his room upstairs and rushed up there to grab him, once again forgetting all about calling Shannon.

CHAPTER TWENTY-FOUR

August 2018

Diane had looked forward to the block party. She had never lived in a neighborhood where they had block parties before, so she was so excited to see what it was all about. Ever since she had discovered the blood on the floor in her house, she hadn't really been able to feel comfortable in her own home, and she had slept outside on the porch, even though it meant she was sweating all through the night. She just didn't like being inside.

She had started to break up the planks and remove them and hoped she could be done this weekend since she had to work all of next week at the motel. The first couple of days working for Jack's parents had been fun and, as usual, Sherri and Albert did their best for her to feel welcome. But she couldn't help feeling like they were doing her a favor. She had kind of known it would end up like that when asking for a job at their place, and to be honest, maybe that was why she had gone to them in the first place. But now that she felt that it was like charity and that maybe Sherri didn't really need her help at all, that she could easily do all that sweeping and cooking on her own, Diane had promised herself to begin looking for another job as soon as she could. The last thing she wanted was to be a burden to Jack's parents. They had always treated her so nicely and, even though Sherri didn't say it out loud, Diane sensed that she had always somehow wished that she and Jack would end up together. Diane got the impression that Sherri wasn't too fond of Jack's new wife, the famous country singer, Shannon King. Not that she didn't like her, but it was the fact that she was away so much and left Jack to deal with everything—and like a million kids—on his own. It bothered Sherri that Shannon wouldn't choose to take care of her family over her career. It wasn't said with those words, but Sherri wasn't very subtle either when speaking about it. Diane feared that Sherri had begun wishing that Diane and Jack would get back together now that she had moved there, but that wasn't why Diane had come to Cocoa Beach. She was in a completely different place emotionally. Diane really didn't want to get in the middle of anything. She just wanted to be left alone and to get on with her life, alone.

"What do you say, Misty?" she said to the cat and picked it up. She was standing on the porch, looking at the decorations she had just put up. Jean had told her it was tradition that everyone decorated their house in whatever manner they liked, so Diane had gone to the beach and picked up tons of shells that she had put on strings and let hang down. She couldn't really afford to go all out in decorations, so she had decided to keep it simple. Her house was a beach house, and now it was visible to everyone. It was also the smallest house on the street and the one that needed the most work. She knew that the neighbors looked at it as an eyesore in their nice neighborhood and wished she had enough money to fix it up properly. But that wasn't now.

"You like it? Looks great, right?"

The cat meowed, then writhed itself out of her hands, jumped down, and ran inside.

"You're right," Diane said with a disappointed

sigh. "It looks terrible. But it's the best I could do. It'll have to be enough. Maybe next year I can do more. Next year, everything will be a lot better."

CHAPTER TWENTY-FIVE

August 2018

No one came to her house. There were enough of them; especially the neighborhood kids were swarming the streets, walking from house to house, escorted by their parents, asking for treats or drinks, asking to see people's houses. It was like Halloween, but with tours of people's houses, Jean had explained. Diane had thought it was a great idea and an amazing way to get to know your neighbors and see how they lived, even though she knew they would be quite disappointed when entering her house. She had cleaned it up as nicely as she could and had prepared a ton of excuses for why half of the floors were ripped up in the kitchen and why everything looked the way it did, but she also believed she had made it look as nice as possible for the occasion. It wasn't half bad if you asked her. She really wanted to make friends in this neighborhood, to make her feel more at home, more settled.

Yet, none of them came to Diane's house.

They would politely wave as they walked past, some would even say hello or hi, then rush past Diane who was standing on the porch with homemade lemonade for the kids and beers for the adults. She even had a bowl of candy to lure them in. Diane knew the way to people's hearts went through their kids.

They just didn't come.

She watched them as they went next door, to the fighting couple, Tim and Tiffany, and Diane could hear them chatting and laughing and making *ooh* and *ah* noises as they were escorted through the house. She saw them walk in and ten minutes later walk back out again, laughing and talking. She saw them come in and out of Dennis and Camille's house across the street and noticed that they usually hung out a little longer at their place than at the others, chatting on the front—newly mowed—lawn, while their kids played in their tree house and on their swing set.

They even went up to Mr. Fogerty's house, and he hadn't even decorated it at all. He hadn't even put out any refreshments, and when they asked to see his house, he told them it hadn't changed a bit since last year, so there was no need. And then they left, shivering slightly because of the creepy old man, but at least they had approached him. They didn't even come up to Diane. Not even when she walked into the street and greeted the parents and presented herself. At first, they were all very nice and shook her hand, but as soon as she told them she had moved into the old house, they all seemed to be in a hurry to get out of there, making up some excuse that they were running out of time or something like that.

Diane watched, puzzled, as they went to Mr. Fogerty's house and not hers. All he did was sit there on his porch in that old rocking chair with his dog. He didn't even want to participate, yet they went to him?

What am I doing wrong?

"Is it the decorations?" she asked herself. "Do they frighten people somehow? They're nothing but shells and rocks?"

Just as she had asked herself that very question, she spotted Jean approaching in the next crowd coming along. As usual, she was holding that Yeti cup in her hand, which Diane assumed contained something a lot stronger than coffee.

Diane waved at her and yelled her name.

"Hi, Jean."

As she saw that the group she was with kept walking and continued past her house without even looking her way, Diane rushed up to Jean and stopped her.

"Hi. What's up?" Jean asked, taking a sip from her cup.

The crowd continued without her.

"Why isn't anyone stopping at my house?" Diane asked. "Is it something I have said or done?"

Jean took another sip, then looked at her pensively. "You really don't know, do ya'?"

"I really, really don't," Diane said.

Jean pulled Diane aside, then exhaled. "I am afraid that they don't dare to go into your house."

Diane wrinkled her forehead. "That's just silly. Why?"

"Well…" she sighed. "I hate to have to be the one to tell ya' this, but an entire family was murdered in your house once. Slaughtered. Most of the folks that live here now weren't even here back then, but they've heard the story. They're scared, Diane."

Diane stared at Jean. "Then how come I haven't?"

"Well, you're from outta town. They're not really obligated to tell ya' when they sell you the house. No one's gonna tell ya' you're about to buy a murder house. At least not till you've signed on the dotted line. But it's your house now, Diane. It's all yours."

PART TWO

CHAPTER TWENTY-SIX

August 2018

Jenna had always known she wanted to be a nurse. She wanted to take care of people and had been doing it ever since she was a child and her mother was diagnosed with thyroid cancer. Jenna had been fifteen years old, and since her mother was all she had, she had nursed her for all of the six months she had been bedridden, while the cancer slowly ate her up.

It was a dark period in Jenna's life, one she didn't enjoy looking back on, but it had also been the time when she had realized her true calling in life. Bringing comfort to her mother made sense to her; it gave her a purpose in all the darkness. In that way, she felt like she had done everything she could and been there for her mother as much as she could before she left.

Today, when she took care of her patients at Cape Canaveral Hospital, she felt the same way. She was no doctor and couldn't cure them or perform surgery, but she could bring comfort. She could make their time here at the hospital as comfortable as possible and taking care of them put a smile on her face.

Today, as she went to change the fluids on the young coma patient in room 237, she didn't feel her usual happy self, though. Her mind was circling around her daughter and the fact that she had been held back and had to retake fourth grade this school year. It was such a huge disappointment for her, and a blow for her daughter's self-confidence. It was just plain cruel, Jenna thought. Now all her daughter's friends were in fifth grade. They were moving on while her daughter had to repeat everything she learned last year among kids that were much younger and less mature than her. It just wasn't fair, and Jenna didn't feel like the school had been very cooperative.

Jenna had tried to fight the school as soon as they told her in the spring that they were considering holding her daughter back. Jenna's daughter had terrible self-esteem as it was and often doubted herself so much she didn't even want to go to school. It was a fight every morning to get her even to go since she believed she was too dumb to learn, so naturally, Jenna argued that this would make things worse. Her daughter was an introvert and had trouble making new friends. Didn't they understand that? Wasn't there another way they could help her?

But she had failed her FSA test, and since her grades from the rest of the year weren't that great, they had no choice, the principal had told her. She gave her one more chance to improve during summer school, but unfortunately, that wasn't enough. It had been so close, the teacher said, but not enough. She had to retake fourth grade. There was nothing more they could do to help her.

"You just don't want to," Jenna had said, then walked out of the teacher's classroom.

Now she wondered how her daughter would cope with this new reality. Would the other kids mock her for it? Call her slow or even stupid? Kids could be so cruel.

"Poor baby," Jenna mumbled to herself as she

smiled at the handsome officer guarding the coma patient's door, then pushed it open.

The sight that met her on the other side almost caused her to drop the bag of fluids and, for just a few seconds, she forgot all about her daughter as she rushed down the hallway yelling for the doctor.

CHAPTER TWENTY-SEVEN

August 2018

Shannon was sitting in her dressing room, looking at the flowers in front of her. They looked like they were exactly the same as the last city they had been in, she thought to herself.

Her hand was hurting even worse than ever, and tears were running down her cheeks as she held it in pain. Between sobs, she glanced at the guitar in the corner, knowing that in a few hours she was supposed to hold it again, on stage, while thousands of fans expected her to give them her all.

It made her feel like screaming.

Shannon had never felt lonelier than she did at this moment. Jack hadn't called her back, and she was tired of calling him and getting his voicemail.

Didn't they miss her at all? Was she that easy to forget?

He's just busy. With the kids and his case. You know that, silly.

She did. But still, she couldn't help wondering if he was with her, that Diane woman who had somehow taken over her life back home.

Shannon leaned back in the couch and cursed the flowers. Whose idea was it anyway to send her all of those? Did they assume she liked them? Shannon did like flowers, she loved flowers, and she might have mentioned that in some interview once, but not when she had to look at them every day. Not when every bloody city, every stadium, and every dressing room had them. Now they just reminded her of her loneliness.

There was a discreet tap on the door and Shannon's manager, Bruce, poked his head in.

"Hey there. How's my star? I have someone here to see you."

Behind him, a face appeared, and the person walked in. Shannon looked at him, surprised.

"Dr. Stanton? What are you doing here? On a Sunday?"

Dr. Stanton had been her physician when she lived in Nashville, but she hadn't seen him in years.

He was one that many celebrities, especially singers, used and she had been very fond of him back then.

He glanced at her hand that she was holding in a strange position.

"I came to look at that."

Shannon looked down at her hand, then wiped away tears. "How did you…?"

She spotted Sarah behind the doctor and didn't need to finish her question. "Ah…I see."

"I'm sorry," Shannon, she said. "I just…I can't keep watching you in pain like that. I know you've been trying to hide it, but I am a mama, and I can see when someone isn't right. And you ain't right, girl. You're in pain. And every time I mention seeing someone about it, you won't hear of it. I feel bad for ambushing you like this, but something has to happen. I can't stand watching you trying to pretend like you're not hurting."

"Can I at least have a look at it?" Doctor Stanton said and put his bag on the table next to the flowers. Just the smell from them made Shannon want to gag.

She nodded. "Sure."

Sarah let out a sigh of relief behind him, and Shannon gave her a look. She was annoyed with her for interfering, but deep down she felt great relief.

Dr. Stanton touched her hand, and she winced in pain.

"That bad, huh?" he asked, concerned.

"It's worse," she said. "And I have to play in just a few hours."

The doctor studied her hand some more, then looked at her. "I'm glad I was called. There's no way you can play when you're in that much pain."

"Can you make her ready for the stage in just two hours?" Bruce asked nervously.

Dr. Stanton gave Shannon a reassuring look. "Without a doubt. I'll get you through tonight and the rest of this tour; don't you worry."

CHAPTER TWENTY-EIGHT

August 2018

I drove the truck up in front of her house, dragging the trailer behind it, and parked. Then I sounded the horn till Diane came out, a surprised look on her face. I got out and greeted her. Mike Wagner was with me and got out on the other side. He nodded at the neighbor across the street who was mowing his lawn and staring at us.

"Jack? What are you doing?" Diane asked, puzzled.

"Bringing you furniture."

"What? Where...What do you mean furniture?"

"I mean just that," I said and walked to the back of the U-HAUL trailer. I opened the hatch and walked up. "There are two couches, an old dining room table and four chairs, and most importantly… a bed."

"I…I…what…?"

"Now, most of it is old stuff that my parents had at the motel and weren't using anymore, like the dining table and the dresser, but they still work. The couches are some we had in the garage. They're actually my old couches from my apartment. Shannon didn't care for them, so they ended up in our garage. We don't need them. Now, about the bed. The frame is old, but I bought you a brand-new mattress. I hope you don't mind."

Diane stared at me, then at the contents of the trailer, then back at me again. "Oh, I also threw in a couple of old lamps that we don't use anymore."

"This…oh, Jack…this is awfully nice, but you really…shouldn't…" she said.

"Ah, it's nothing. Really. It isn't. I went around the house yesterday and realized we had so much stuff we never use. I thought, why not share some of it with someone who needs it. You can't keep sleeping on the porch on that old mattress there."

"But…well…how can I…"

"…say no? You can't."

I smiled from ear to ear. It brought me tremendous joy to help her out, and I wasn't kidding or being modest. It really wasn't much.

Diane smiled now too as she took it all in.

"Then, thank you, Jack."

"Ah, thank me later. Now, let's get all this stuff inside before the thunderstorms get here. Now, I brought my colleague, Mike. He's happy to help, aren't you, Mike?"

"Sure am," Mike said and smiled.

"When I told him on Friday that you were sleeping on the porch, he was the one who told me we needed to do something. Isn't that right, Mike?"

"Sure is," Mike said.

"Mike's also the sergeant at the station, a good person to know around here," I added, while we went into the trailer and started to carry out the small things, like the lamps, first.

Next, Mike and I grabbed the mattress and placed it inside. Diane had ripped up all of the wooden planks in the kitchen by now and had started putting in the tiles. I was quite impressed with her craftsmanship. It was rare in a woman. I knew Shannon wouldn't be able to change a light bulb on her own.

Shannon! You've got to call her!

I decided to do it on my way back. Things had just been so hectic all weekend with Tyler being sick and all. Shannon would understand as soon as I explained it all to her. She would want me to help someone like Diane out and, once I explained to her why I hadn't called back, she'd forgive me. I knew she would.

"Where are the kids?" Diane asked as we put the couch down in her living room. "It's Sunday; they're not in school?"

"They're hanging out with my parents," I said. "My mom's looking after Tyler. His fever came down last night, and we actually got some sleep. Today, he was back to running around and being his old spectacular self."

"That's good news, Jack," Diane said.

I looked around, then clapped my hands.

"Now, all we need is to put up the bed. Mike, you wanna give me a hand with the mattress and get it upstairs?"

We grabbed the mattress at each end when someone came up to the open door. Diane went to him. He was holding a huge bouquet of flowers between his hands and wore a shirt that said BEACHSIDE FLORIST.

"That's nice," I said. "Someone sent you flowers?"

Diane looked at the man, then at the flowers. He handed them to her, and she took them, even though it was a little reluctantly. The man told us to *have a nice day,* then rushed back to his car, leaving Diane inside holding the flowers between her hands.

"Daisies, huh?" I said and let go of the mattress. I walked to her. "Who are they from?"

She shook her head. "It doesn't say."

"There's no card?" I asked.

She looked up and our gaze met. "No."

"That's odd. Could they be from someone you met around here?" I asked.

"I…I don't think…I've barely met anyone."

"Could it be the wrong house?" Mike asked and wiped his sweaty fingers on his shorts.

Diane stared at the flowers, and I noticed her hands holding them were shaking. She stood like that for a few seconds, then sniffled and walked outside with the flowers and threw them in the trash. She came back in with a deep exhale.

"I'm allergic to daisies," she said and closed the door. She smiled, but the smile didn't reach her eyes. It stopped short, and her lips started to vibrate nervously. I sensed we needed to leave her alone with this. This was none of our business.

"I have to get back soon. How about that mattress?" I said, addressed to Mike. "Let's get it up the stairs."

He helped me get it up, and we set up the bed for her, then walked down the stairs, where Diane was arranging everything else.

"Now, would you look at that?" I said. "It almost looks like a real home now."

Diane smiled, and this time it was a real smile.

"Thank you so much. You have no idea how big a help this is."

I hugged her. "No problem. I was glad to help. So was Mike, right Mike?"

"Sure was."

We walked to the truck and got in. As the engine roared to a start and I was about to take off, Mike took one last look at the house.

"You do know what house that is, right?"

I shook my head. "No."

Mike whistled. "It's been empty for years. I bet no one told her what happened there. No one else would buy that place. Not if they knew."

I stared at him, remembering the blood on the

planks. "You mean murder? Someone was killed in that house?"

Mike scoffed. "Look up the Carver case when you get to the station tomorrow. And don't do it right before lunch. You won't have an appetite for a little while afterward."

CHAPTER TWENTY-NINE

August 2018

I went back to the house before going to pick up the kids. They all needed to shower before school tomorrow, and I had to make lunches for them all and sign their planners and make sure they had done their homework, if they had any. But right now, I just wanted to enjoy a few minutes of quiet before the chaos set in.

So, I called Shannon. Finally, I had the break I needed to be able to talk to her properly. It wasn't that I didn't want to talk to her, I desperately did, but I wanted to talk to her when there was time to, not while three kids screamed in my ear or right before she went on stage. I didn't want to rush it; I wanted to talk to her properly and really feel her.

"Hello? Jack?"

"Shannon!"

"Hey! How is everything? How are the kids?"

I chuckled. She sounded happy. There was nothing better in the world than a happy Shannon. It was just like the kids. If everyone was happy, then I was too. If Shannon was happy, then I was in heaven.

"They're great. They're at the motel."

"Why aren't they with you at the house?" she asked. "Don't tell me you're working on a Sunday."

"Why not? You are," I said with another chuckle.

"Jack."

"Of course, I'm not working. Mike and I just took some furniture to Diane's place. Can you believe she had none? I took my old couches from the garage, the ones you can't stand, and then some stuff from my parents' place that they didn't use anymore. Oh, and the old bedframe too. The one leaning up against the wall in the garage behind everything."

Shannon went silent.

"You did what?"

"I gave some furniture to Diane. You remember

her, right? She didn't have any, so I gave her some that we don't use. You don't mind, do you?"

More silence. "No. Of course not."

It came a little hesitantly, and I knew I had screwed up. I closed my eyes. Shannon had trust issues. How could I be so stupid? She knew I used to date Diane and, even though I didn't think about it or about her in that way—in any way—of course, Shannon would think I did. Of course, she would feel threatened by her since she wasn't here.

"Shannon…I was just helping her out. I don't know what she's running from, but I have a feeling she might be in trouble. You should see the house she's bought. It's awful, and now Mike tells me that once someone was murdered in that house. I feel sorry for her, Shannon, that's all."

Shannon was quiet for a little while, then she said with a weak and scratchy voice:

"Of course. Jack Ryder to the rescue, right?"

"That's not fair, Shannon, and you know it."

Silence again. It was killing me.

Say something, Shannon; just say anything.

"Listen, I have a concert soon. I should go get ready. Talk to you later, all right? Tell the kids I miss them."

And without even letting me protest, she hung up.

CHAPTER THIRTY

August 2018

"He's awake."

It was Joe on the phone. I had barely hung up—and cursed myself for being an insensitive fool toward Shannon—when he called.

"Parker Reynolds," he said. "He woke up."

"You're kidding me?" I said while looking at my watch. The kids could easily stay at their grandparents' place for a few more hours till we had to start all the routine stuff to get them ready for school tomorrow.

"I'll meet you there," I said.

I rushed to the car and jumped in. Calling the Weasel on the way and filling her in, I drove through downtown Cocoa Beach, careful to stop for a jaywalking tourist. They always seemed to think everyone else had to be on vacation too since they were.

At the hospital, I showed my badge at reception. Not that I needed to since the lady there knew me by now, but more out of formality. I took the elevator up to Parker Reynolds' room.

Joe had been the officer keeping guard outside his room all day, and he greeted me when I arrived.

"He's been awake for a couple of hours," he said, "but the doctors wanted to run all the tests and examine him before they'd let me call you."

"You did good, thanks, Joe," I said and tapped him on the shoulder.

I pushed the door open and went inside. A nurse was there, and so was Jim Reynolds. Parker was sitting up, and the nurse was feeding him soup. Jim Reynolds approached me.

"He just woke up. I won't have you torturing him with all your questions. Let the boy come to himself first, will you?"

I nodded. "I'll go easy on him; don't worry. I just need to talk to him as soon as possible. He is, after all, the only one who has seen the killer."

Jim Reynolds grumbled something I chose not

to hear since it was definitely offensive, but I took no notice. I approached the boy.

"He was hungry," the nurse said, smiling. "It was the first thing he said. And the only thing he's said so far."

I smiled, then nodded.

"Hi there, Parker. How are you doing?"

He swallowed the soup while looking at me.

"I'm not going to bother you with a lot of questions about what happened," I said. "But I do need to know one thing. Did you see him? Did you see his face?"

The boy sighed. "I…I don't really re…"

"He doesn't remember anything," Jim Reynolds took over. "I asked him the same question when he woke up. He remembers nothing from what happened that morning."

"Nothing?" I asked, disappointed.

The boy shook his head with a confused look in his eyes, which I wondered if it could be fear. I glared at him, scrutinizing him. Was it really true? Didn't he remember, or was he just saying so because he was scared?

"All right," I said. "We can talk later; maybe you'll be able to remember something eventually, okay? You just make sure you get better, then I'll work on finding who did this. Just promise me to let me know if you remember anything at all. Anything will do. Like the color of his hair or his size would be of help."

I felt Parker's hand touch mine as I was about to leave, and I turned to look at him. Fear had struck his eyes.

"H-he's still out there?"

I nodded, thinking that for someone who didn't remember anything, he sure seemed frightened.

"Yes, but we will catch him. That is my promise to you."

CHAPTER THIRTY-ONE

August 2018

Josef Carpenter might only have been five years old, but he wasn't too young to get dressed by himself in the mornings. It was a new thing, yes, and his mother wasn't too certain it was a good idea, but Josef wanted to show her that he could. She had put out his clothes for him and, as he put his feet onto the carpet that tickled his toes so delightfully on this Monday morning, he rushed to put them on by himself, making sure he got his shirt on the right way and not end up with the tag in front like last time.

Proud of his accomplishment, Josef looked at himself in the mirror on his wall, next to the piles of Legos that he had forgotten to clean up the night before like his mom had told him to.

"Looking dashing," he told his reflection with a grin. Just like his momma used to say to him when helping him dress.

There was a light knock on his door, and his mother's beautiful face peeked inside.

"How's it going in here, champ? You need any help?"

Josef smiled, his smile reaching all the way to his eyes. His mother exhaled, relieved.

"I guess you don't," she said. "You even put on your shoes by yourself. I am impressed."

"Told you," Josef said, straightening his back.

"Now, come eat. The bus will be here shortly. I have to wake up your brother."

Josef strode to the breakfast counter and sat on a stool. He grabbed the spoon in his Cheerios and started shoveling them in.

"Hey, doofus," his brother, Mark, said as he came out. He ruffled Josef's hair and Josef grumbled, then straightened it with his hand to correct the mess his brother had made.

His brother sat on the stool next to him, then glanced down at Josef's feet with a loud chuckle. He grabbed the cereal box and poured himself some.

"You do realize you're wearing your shoes on the wrong feet, you moron," he said and shook his head while shoveling in his cereal. He was eating it so fast he finished his first bowl before Josef and then poured himself some more. "Mom, have you seen his feet?"

Their mom gave him a look. "At least he put them on by himself. You didn't do that when you were five years old."

"And maybe I like them better this way," Josef said and slid down from his chair. The shoes felt strange and tight in an odd way, but he wasn't going to let his older brother mock him. If Josef wanted to wear his shoes on the wrong feet, then he was entitled to do so.

Josef snorted happily, grabbed his backpack and lunch pack, then walked to his mother and gave her a kiss. They rubbed noses, and his mother looked deeply into his eyes.

"Who's a good boy?" she asked, her green eyes sparkling like jewelry as she spoke.

Josef sighed happily. "I am."

"There you go. Now, go knock them out in Kindergarten."

"I will," Josef said and walked toward the door. "Mrs. Thomas already loves me."

Josef put a hand on the doorknob and turned to take one last glance at his momma. He had insisted on walking to the bus himself, now that he had started real school, and since the bus stopped right outside their house, his momma had let him.

"Have a wonderful day," she said and waved.

"I will," Josef said, turned the doorknob, and opened the door.

As it slid open, a person appeared on the other side. He was wearing a mask, so Josef could see nothing but his eyes. The mask looked like a woman, with its red lips and light, delicate skin.

Thinking it had to be Halloween soon, which was his favorite time of year, Josef stopped and stared at the person approaching his house with a big smile. He didn't even realize the person's intentions before he was pushed back inside the house and the masked person entered along with him.

CHAPTER THIRTY-TWO

My second kill was a lot easier. Not that it was a surprise to me since it was only natural that I would be better prepared, that I would find it easier once I had done it before. Yet, it surprised me how easy it really was. Come to think of it, my second kill was probably the easiest of them all.

I had studied her for weeks, driving up and down her street, keeping a close eye on her. I knew her routines down to the smallest detail. You'd be surprised at just how predictable people really are. People tend to think that they are not, that they are spontaneous and do things differently from day to day, but they really don't. Even their spontaneity is highly predictable.

If you've ever read much about serial killers, then you'll know that they go through what you call phases. One of the phases that they go through is what I call the trolling stage. This is where you're looking for a victim. You can be trolling for months or even years, but once you lock into a certain person, you go from trolling to stalking. Sometimes, there are several of them that you're stalking at the same time, till you finally decide on the one. While stalking her, you lock in on her every move. You almost become like one with her. That's what it was like with this woman.

The more I know about a person, the more comfortable I feel about what I am about to do. And I knew a lot about this one. I had been watching her, stalking her for a few weeks, going to her work, meeting her on the street, even walking to her door and talking to her, sizing her up. I knew very early on that she would be the one. There was no avoiding it. So, I just selected a day to do it. I usually like doing it in the daylight, often in the mornings when the victims have just woken up. People tend to be a lot more trusting at that time of day. They don't seem to think a bad thing can happen as supposed to at night when it is dark out. But I am here to tell you; it can happen at any hour of the day. I don't need darkness to cover me up.

The woman lived alone with her children, which is usually preferable. Men tend to mess up the picture. They're stronger, and they fight for their lives and the lives of their loved ones a lot more ferociously. I like it if the woman has children. They're usually very easy to handle and deal with, especially the young ones. They're gullible. I don't mind killing children, but I am not coming for them. It's the mothers, the women I prefer. I come for the women.

I came while she was at work. I parked my car a few blocks away, then walked to her house. I rang the doorbell first, holding the bowling bag with my kill-kit in my hand. I called it my kill-kit. Thought that was pretty clever.

The reason I rang the doorbell wasn't because I expected her to open the door but to make sure she wasn't home. Just in case. And, as I had figured, she was at work. So instead, I walked around the back, found the back door, and opened it. Like so many people, she had a spare key hidden right above the door. I had seen her place it there, so it was no problem for me to find it. Again, people are so predictable; it's almost scary.

Inside her house, I hid in the closet till she came home. It took about an hour till I finally heard the front door slam shut and the footsteps approach. I waited in that closet and listened while she and her children had dinner, and later when she put them to bed and sang to them. The moment she entered the bedroom to change out of her uniform, I considered making myself known, but I wanted to stick with the plan, so I waited. If she opened the closet, then I would attack. I would have to, but I was so hoping she wouldn't. And she didn't. She threw her uniform on the chair next to the bed and got herself ready to go to sleep. I waited all night and listened to her breathing. It wasn't until the next morning when she woke up and went to get her underwear that I jumped out of the closet, wearing my mask.

CHAPTER THIRTY-THREE

August 2018

The person who had entered Josef's house closed the door behind him, locked it, then rushed to the windows, turned down the blinds, and shut off the TV. And that was when he showed Josef the gun in his hand. Josef stared at it, then at his mother, who was standing in the kitchen and had dropped the gallon of milk in her hand. The milk was gushing out from the plastic container onto the tiles, but she didn't even notice. Josef's big brother, Mark, stood like he was frozen, while a dark spot emerged on the crotch of his jeans, seeping through the fabric.

The masked person pointed the gun at them, then spoke.

"Put the children in the bathroom and close the door. Now."

Josef's mother whimpered. She had left the fridge open, and it was now making that annoying noise to tell her so. She shut it, then ran to Mark and Josef and grabbed them by their necks. "Come with me, boys. Hurry."

"But…Mom?" Josef whined.

His mother pushed him toward the bathroom. "I'll be fine. Don't worry. Just get in there. Now."

Mark obeyed and hurried inside the bathroom, where he sat on the toilet bowl, his legs shaking, whereas Josef hesitated. He started to cry and held onto his mother.

"I don't wanna go, Momma. I wanna be with you, Momma; I wanna stay here with you."

"Just do as I tell you to, and we'll all be fine," his mother said, but even to a five-year-old, her words weren't very convincing. "Now, go. Lock the door after you."

"But…but Momma…" Josef wailed, but his mother didn't want to hear any more. She pushed the boy inside the bathroom, then slammed the door shut.

Josef screamed and sprang for the handle, but

she held it closed. Mark then rushed up and locked it, using the hatch high up that Josef couldn't reach.

"Momma! Momma! Momma!" Josef screamed and hammered on the door as hard as he could, till the blood was pounding in his hands.

After that, he slid to the cold tiles, crying. Behind the door, he could hear the masked person and his momma speaking.

"What do you want?" his momma asked. "Is it money? I have some stashed in the bedroom. In the back of my closet. You can take all of it, if only you spare our lives. At least the children."

"I am not here for money," the voice behind the mask answered.

"Then why are you here?" Josef's mother asked. Her voice was shivering the same way it had when the doctor at the hospital had told her that Josef's dad wasn't going to wake up again after he had fallen in the bathroom. It was his heart, they said. It happens, they also said. It was one of the few things Josef remembered from that time since he had only been four years old. But his mother's shivering voice when she spoke to the doctors while thinking he was too young to understand, he would never forget.

"You…y-you want sex?"

The man behind the mask started to laugh. It was a sound so chilling, it made Josef feel cold.

"I am not here for sex either, no," the masked person said.

"T-then why are you here?"

"Let me get you a glass of water to calm you down," he said. "You're getting upset."

Josef could hear him open the cabinet and grab a glass. He then heard the water run from the fridge.

"Here," the masked man said.

Next followed a silence and Josef was certain he could hear his mother drinking the water, but maybe he was just imagining it. Josef calmed down a little when realizing that this guy was being nice to his mother, that he was actually being nice to her. Maybe he didn't want to be mean to them? Maybe he was actually a nice man?

Josef breathed a sigh of relief when the glass was put down on something, probably the counter. Josef looked at his brother sitting on top of the toilet bowl. He had pulled his legs up under his chin and was shaking, staring blankly into the air.

Josef felt like comforting him. He wanted to tell him it was going to be all right. This guy didn't want money or…sex. He had just given their mother a glass of water, and he spoke very calmly and didn't yell at all or anything, not like that guy living down the street who had yelled at Josef for skateboarding in front of his house. He was nothing like him, and that was good, 'cause that guy was mean. He was really mean. This guy was nothing like that.

But Josef didn't get to open his mouth and utter the words before he heard something else coming from the other side of the door. The words that fell —and felt like someone ripped out Josef's heart— came from the masked man.

"I'm here to kill you."

Josef rose to his feet as he heard thudding and thumping noises from the other side of the door. Groaning and bumps were followed by muffled screams. It sounded exactly like when Mark occasionally would put a pillow over Josef's head and hold him down until their mother intervened.

The sounds made Mark stop whimpering and walk to the door. He put an ear to it, and they listened to their mother fighting for her life. When the fighting stopped, they both began screaming.

Josef screamed his momma's name so loudly it hurt his own ears, while Mark sank to his knees. In the distance, their mother's cell phone rang. Josef slammed his fists into the door when suddenly there was a scratching noise coming from the other side, and he stopped. Josef stared at the door. He was barely breathing, and his legs were threatening to give in beneath him. Then he felt a warm gust of air coming through the keyhole and brushing his arm. He heard what sounded like heavy breathing. It reminded Josef of that sound that the evil guy made when breathing behind his black mask in those old Jedi-movies that his brother had made him watch, even though their mother had told him Josef wasn't old enough.

Josef gasped, then approached the keyhole and peeked out of it. On the other side, an eye was looking back at him, one that was steel grey like a wolf's. Josef pulled back, shaking, as the man on the other side whispered:

"Remember. You were the one who let me in. You're the one who opened the door for me. Don't you ever forget that, my boy."

CHAPTER THIRTY-FOUR

August 2018

I looked at the mountain of lunchboxes in front of me, then wondered when exactly my life had come to this.

With a deep sigh, I turned to look at my crew of kids, who were eating breakfast. I had gotten up at five thirty to make them pancakes and bacon and to make all the lunches. It wasn't even seven o'clock, and already I was exhausted. I still had an entire workday ahead of me.

I was going to need a lot of coffee.

It didn't help much that I had slept terribly. I kept tossing and turning, thinking about Shannon. I had tried to call her again later in the evening before bedtime when I thought her concert was done for the night, but she hadn't answered. She was probably partying with her manager, publicist, and the press at some fancy after-party.

As Austin and Abigail broke into yet another fight, their third this morning, I couldn't help but envy Shannon. She was out there in the world, being catered to and having her every need met. They even had fresh flowers put out for her every time she entered the dressing room of a new stadium, she had told me. She got pampered at nice restaurants and lived in hotels where she didn't even have to do her own laundry. Meanwhile, I was drowning in dirty shorts and this morning Abigail had yelled at me for not having her favorite shirt clean in time for her to wear.

"I always wear my red surf-shirt on Mondays," she had said. "Always. Now I have nothing to wear! Do you want me to go to school naked?"

I had found the shirt in the bottom of one of the piles, then smelled it. There were no stains on it, but it did smell kind of moldy. I then grabbed one of Shannon's perfumes and sprayed it all over the shirt, then handed it to Abigail. "Here. I'll wash it later."

She had answered with a grunt, then put on the shirt, and now I was looking at her in the crinkled shirt, soaked in perfume so bad that it was stinking up the entire house and made Austin hold his nose —which they were now arguing about.

What have I become?

As the clock turned seven-ten, each of the kids grabbed their lunches and trotted out the door where the school bus picked them up. Tyler and I stood in the front yard and waved at them, me secretly breathing in relief. I had survived yet another of these chaotic mornings. That, in itself, was quite the accomplishment.

"Now that they're all gone, we can have a nice, quiet breakfast before I take you to the preschool," I said and put him down.

We held each other's hands and walked back inside, where we were met by a mess of plates with half-eaten pancakes. A glass of orange juice was tipped over and had spilled all over the counter and even soaked a roll of paper towels. Some of it was dripping onto the floor and had left a small puddle.

Tyler giggled and ran to his toys that he had thrown in a pile in the living room, while I made myself some much-needed coffee.

CHAPTER THIRTY-FIVE

She asked me if she could smoke a cigarette first. I had tied her up, but the request was so unusual, I agreed to let her do it. Just so she would know she was at my mercy. Maybe she thought she could appeal to me like that, maybe talk me out of my intentions, and I decided to play along with it for a little while, mostly for my amusement. I forgot to tell her that I don't have a softer side. It is funny, though, how people often think they can talk their way out of me killing them. As if the decision hadn't already been made long ago. As if I had a choice not to kill them. What they don't seem to understand is that I am not human. Not the way they are. I am a freak of nature. A mistake. And the only way to stop me is to put me down.

The woman I was about to kill sat in the kitchen, smoking, breathing in puffs, her hands shaking heavily while we talked. I told her all the things I would do to her and, to my surprise, she didn't even try to escape or scream. She simply nodded while smoking. As she killed the cigarette in the ashtray and blew out the last of the smoke, she turned her head and looked at me. It was so beautiful. Like she gave herself to me.

And then I killed her.

I wrapped a plastic bag around her head, then tied a rope around her neck, and tightened it. I looked into her eyes as she fought to breathe. And then I killed her children the same way.

I was never happier than in those moments when I killed someone. It doesn't last long, unfortunately, but it is by far the most satisfying feeling in the world. There's nothing like it. People jump out of planes, or off bridges or they climb mountains or jump from helicopters onto mountaintops where from they ski, but I doubt any of them ever had a thrill ride quite like the one I had in those days.

In the days that followed, I was on everyone's lips. Everywhere, the police looked for me. Everywhere, they spoke of me with those fearful eyes and shivering voices. Now that I had finished my second kill, they knew they had to be dealing with a serial killer, and they started making up names for me. The Cocoa Beach Strangler some TV station came up with, but that wasn't quite sticking with the public. But later, a local newspaper came up with the name The Monday

Morning Killer, since I had made both of my first kills on Monday mornings. The name had stuck with me since then. And I kind of liked it. Once they gave me that name, I was naturally obligated to honor that. So, from then on, all my kills took place on Monday mornings.

CHAPTER THIRTY-SIX

August 2018

By the time I reached my office at the station, I was on my fourth cup of coffee. Tyler had been acting up all the way to the daycare. He didn't want to go today; he wanted to stay home and play with his dinosaur toys. I had to carry him in there, screaming and crying, and just hand him to his teacher. Luckily, she was very good with him, and after much talking, he finally let go of my hair. I told the teacher he was just acting out because he missed his mom, and she gave me an understanding and very sympathetic look while tilting her head slightly to the side. I was getting looks like those a lot lately. Especially from women.

At the station, I went through my interview with

Jim Reynolds again, watching it on my screen, studying his every movement and grimace. I couldn't quite figure the guy out. What was his deal?

By the time we reached mid-morning, I decided I deserved one of those tasty pastry treats that our secretary, Elyse, had brought in today. Sugar and caffeine combined should do the trick. I had barely sunk my teeth into it when Weasel came toward me, her eyes somber.

"Ryder. I need you. We have a situation."

I dropped the pastry and put down the coffee. I grabbed my badge and gun, then rushed after her out to one of the patrol cars. She turned on the engine, and we roared onto A1A, sirens blaring.

"What's up?" I asked. "Where are we going?"

"Park Lane. North side of town. A neighbor called it in this morning. He was out walking the dog when he heard screaming coming from a house. A patrol car went out there and found a woman dead in the living room."

"Yikes."

Weasel accelerated the car and turned onto Park Lane. She stopped the car in front of a house where two other police cars were parked as well.

She turned the engine off and looked at me with a sigh.

"We need someone who's good with kids."

"Kids?" I asked as we got out and rushed toward the house. We walked inside, and I spotted the body first before I heard the screams. Weasel stopped in front of a bathroom door.

"Kid. Locked himself in there. He doesn't dare to come out. He's too terrified."

She gave me a friendly look. "The scene is all yours."

I took in a deep breath and imagined for a second that it was my own kid behind that door. Tears were piling up behind my eyes as I listened to the intense screaming. I glanced back at the dead body in the living room.

"I take it she was killed?" I asked Weasel.

She nodded. "Plastic bag."

My eyes grew wide. "Like Parker Reynolds' sister?"

Weasel nodded. I looked at the door with a deep exhale. "So, this kid must have heard it all."

"That's what I'm afraid of," she said.

I knelt down by the door and knocked on it, then spoke with a gentle voice.

"This is the police. Who's in there?"

All I got in response was whimpering and more crying. I felt sweat spring to my forehead, worrying about this kid. The screams were excruciating. I couldn't stand the sound of them. I looked in through the keyhole and saw a boy. He was sitting on the floor, had his hands over his head and mouth open like he couldn't stop screaming no matter how hard he tried.

"He must be in shock," I said, addressed to Weasel.

"Poor thing. We have to get him out of there. I don't want to break down the door and scare him further, but I'll do it if I have to."

"Just give me a second," I said and put a hand inside the pocket of my pants. I pulled out a small container.

"What's that?" Weasel said.

I smiled. "Tyler always leaves me a small surprise when I drop him off. He says he wants to make sure I'm not bored at work. I always forget to take it out again."

I knocked on the door and spoke through the screaming.

"Say, anyone up for playing with some slime?"

Finally, the screaming stopped. A few seconds passed, and an eye looked out of the keyhole.

"What kind of slime?" A small voice said with a loud sniffle.

I looked at the container in my hand. "I actually believe this is thinking putty."

"What color is it?" the voice asked.

"Purple, I think. But you'll have to come out here to really see. The light is better out here. It has sparkles in it and everything." I squeezed the thinking putty in my hand and made sure he could see it.

"It feels really good. If you come out, I'll let you hold it and squeeze it," I said and let the purple mass squeeze out between my fingers, pretending like it was awesome. Reality was, I hated any slime or putty that my kids ever owned or made themselves. It somehow always ended up in the carpet or someone's hair. The feeling itself made me squirm. But I knew all kids liked it, no matter the age.

A few seconds passed, and my eyes met Weasel's.

"You sure you're police?"

I showed him my badge through the keyhole. "Sure am. My name is Jack. What's your name?"

"I…I…" the boy looked behind himself anxiously, then back at me.

Someone is with him, I mouthed to Weasel. *He's not alone.*

She nodded.

"It's okay," I said. "I'm not going to hurt you. But if you tell me your name, it'll make it easier to talk to you. I prefer to know who I am talking to, don't you? 'Cause our mommas told us to never talk to strangers, right?"

The boy thought for a few seconds more. His eyes were on the putty in my hand. I held it up to the keyhole, feeling slightly like I was luring the child, like some abductor, but it was the only way to get him to come out without having to use force and scare the crap out of him again.

"I…I am Josef," the small voice said.

"Okay, Josef," I said. "Now we know each other. We are no longer strangers. Now, can you open the door for me, Josef?"

"I…I c-can't reach," he said. "It's too high up."

"Okay. Now, are you alone in there?"

"N-no."

"Who's in there with you?" I asked. "Josef?"

He looked out of the keyhole again.

"Who is in there?"

"My…my brother," he said.

"Your brother, huh? And what's his name?"

"M-Mark."

I nodded. "All right, and what is your brother doing right now?"

The boy looked behind him, then back at me. "H-he is just sitting there. On the toilet." Josef wiped his nose and eyes with his sleeve. He was hoarse from all the screaming. "Staring."

"So, Mark is just sitting on the toilet, staring?" I asked. "How long has he been doing that?"

"S-s-since Mo-o-mma…s-since s-she…"

"What happened to your momma, Josef?" I asked, knowing very well I had to tread carefully here. But if the boy was able to talk about it, then it would be best to do it now while his memory was still fresh.

"Josef?"

No answer. He wasn't able to talk about it after all.

"Have you been hurt, Josef?" I asked.

"N-no."

"Your brother? Is he hurt?"

"It was only…M-omma…"

"What happened to her? Do you know?"

But Josef couldn't talk anymore. I could tell he was losing it and glanced at Weasel, who gave me the go-ahead.

"I need you to step away from the door," I said. "Can you do that for me, Josef?"

I only got a sniffle for an answer, but through the keyhole, I could tell he had moved away. Then I kicked the door as hard as I could. The door came down with a crash, and I managed to get inside just in time. Josef's small body was shaking badly, and then it was like the air simply went out of him, and he fell forward. I jumped ahead and grabbed him in my arms, pulling him up and into my embrace. It was like holding a dead body. There was no life in him, no fight, not even crying. He had gone completely numb.

I sent Weasel a look, and she came inside as well, then spotted Mark who was sitting on top of the toilet, his knees under his chin, rocking back and forth, not even blinking.

Weasel reached down and grabbed him in her arms and, once again, I was amazed at her almost supernatural strength.

"The ambulance is ready for them outside," Mike said coming up to me. "I'll show you to it."

CHAPTER THIRTY-SEVEN

Cocoa Beach 2011

They were fighting. It was an everyday event now. The boy usually sat in his room with his ear placed to the door, listening in on them yelling at one another.

It was because Father had changed. Exactly when it had happened, the boy wasn't certain. But, one day, it was like his dad had simply decided that keeping Momma happy wasn't all it was cracked up to be. It wasn't the most important thing in the world anymore.

The boy just wished that Daddy would have told him when things changed. All his life, he had believed this to be the truth, to be his mission. Keeping Momma happy. And his sister, of course, because if she was happy, Momma was happy. But now things were different, apparently. Now it was more like his dad tried to irritate Momma as much as possible. Like every time she asked him to do something, he would end up yelling at her instead of getting the thing done. It confused the boy since there was nothing worse in the world to him than people yelling. It didn't matter if it was the teacher at school, his sister, some silly neighbor, or even worse, his momma. It felt awful when the boy did things wrong, and he could never get things right, could he? Not according to his mother. She always told him he was in the way. She always shushed him and told him to go to his room or to a friends' house.

"Don't just hang around here and do nothing, you lazy boy," she would say. She especially didn't like it if he left anything around the house, like if he put down his backpack in the hallway and forgot to take it to his room when he walked up the stairs. She would yell at him from down the stairs and tell him that if he didn't come and pick it up now, she'd throw it in the trash.

Now, the boy's backpack wasn't exactly valuable, so it wasn't that he cared so much about it. It was old and worn out, and he had had it since Kindergarten because his mother wouldn't buy him a new one, even though there was a big hole on the bottom of it. Because little sister needed new shoes. She was growing so fast that Momma could hardly keep up with her, she would say and tickle the girl's tummy, while the boy would look at them together and want to scream. His momma had once tickled him like that. Before little sister came to his world. But since then, she hadn't touched him, except to give him a spanking that time when he broke her favorite old clock that she had inherited from her grandmother.

"I'm telling ya', I'm done listening to this," he heard his father yell from the living room downstairs. "You're crazy, woman. Insane. Do you know that?"

"You're the one who's crazy," sounded her reply. "Coming here and thinking you can just…"

"Just what?" his dad said.

"God, I hate you," she snorted.

"Well, the feeling is mutual."

The boy listened while tears rolled across his cheeks and his stomach turned to knots. There truly was nothing worse than people fighting. If he ever became president, he would make fighting illegal.

The boy listened intently and realized the

yelling had finally stopped. He opened his eyes wondering if it was finally over when he heard the door downstairs slam shut. He knew it had to be his father who had stormed out. His mother would never leave the house like that.

Last time they had a fight, his dad had stayed away for two days, and once he came back home, he talked funny, and his eyes looked weird. The boy hadn't liked that.

Now, as he stared at the wall in front of him, the boy wondered how many days it was going to take this time before his dad returned.

The boy stood to his feet and cautiously ran down the stairs, hoping and praying his momma wouldn't see him and take the last bit of her rage out on him, then he stormed into the yard and into the enclosure where he spent the rest of the day with Victoria and Hector, in the only place on earth where he felt truly at home.

CHAPTER THIRTY-EIGHT

August 2018

"The kids are okay," I said and threw the file on the table in front of me and sat down. Weasel handed me a cup of coffee. I sent her a friendly smile. It had been a long day so far, and I was exhausted. My mom had promised to pick up Tyler from daycare and pick the rest of them up by the bus stop and take them to the motel since I had no idea when this day would be over.

"Or should I say, unharmed. The kids are unharmed, but far from okay," I said and sipped my cup.

Weasel sighed and leaned forward in her chair. Mike and Joe were both very quiet. I couldn't blame them. I didn't feel much like talking either, but we had to gather everything we had. Looking into the eyes of those poor kids almost made me lose my composure. Josef had clung onto me and refused to let go of me while the doctor examined him. I had held his poor little hand through it all and felt him trembling at the smallest sound. His brother Mark had finally opened up to me and had told me the most terrifying story.

"So, what we know now," I said, remembering what he had told me earlier, "is that a person forced himself inside the home of Josef and Mark Carpenter, where they lived with their mother, Betty Carpenter. There was no dad in the picture. He died about a year ago. This person—who was wearing a mask of a woman's face with red lipstick and fair skin—entered through the front door when the youngest, Josef, was about to leave for the school bus. He pushed the boy inside and forced himself in with him, where he told the mother to put the boys in the bathroom. From in there, the two children heard the person give their mother a glass of water before he…" I looked down at the papers in front of me while searching for the words. "Before he killed her by placing a plastic bag over her head and tightening it with her own belt. Now, we don't have the autopsy yet, but it's fair to say the cause of death is strangulation. The killer then approached the bathroom door and told one of the children that he wanted him to remember that he was the one who had let him into the house. Mark furthermore told us that his mother's phone rang right before the killer left the house and when we checked the phone, she had several missed calls between six-fifty and seven-thirty. It was her sister who called to see if Betty had time for coffee this afternoon. She was going to tell her that she was pregnant, her sister told me when I spoke to her at the hospital. She has also told us that she is willing to take the boys once they are discharged from the hospital. We do, however, believe that the killer was distracted by the phone ringing and that was why he left the kids unharmed."

"Guess it was their luck," Mike said.

Luck was probably a strong word to use, I thought to myself, but I didn't say anything.

"So, is it fair to say that we have a serial killer in our town then?" Joe Hall said. "I mean, it has to be the same guy that attacked the Reynolds family, right?"

I nodded. "That's what I'm afraid of, yes. There are a lot of similarities in his MO. The use of plastic bags, the fact that he struck a family in the morning hours, and so on. I'm even thinking that maybe he meant to leave the kids, or at least one of them like he did in the first case. Maybe he wanted one left behind to tell the tale. Like Parker was left unharmed."

"So, who is he targeting?" Weasel asked.

"So far, single mothers with their children," I said. "It might indicate he has an issue with women, or maybe they're just easier. You know, when there's no man around. I do think the first is more likely. According to Mark, he was a big guy, tall."

"It kind of reminds me of the case from back in seventy-four," Mike said and leaned forward in his chair.

"Seventy-four?" I said and realized I had forgotten that Mike had been around for a very long time.

"The case I told you about the other day. Did you ever check that out?" he continued. "We called him the Monday Morning Killer."

"I've heard about him," Weasel said. "I lived up north back then, but we even heard about the Monday Morning Killer up there. Geez, I must have been a teenager. Everyone talked about that guy."

"It all started in that house your little girlfriend moved into," Mike said.

"Diane?"

He nodded. "The family who lived there were his first victims. You never heard of him?"

I shook my head, and so did Joe Hall. "I…really haven't…"

Mike rolled his eyes. "Geez, you guys are young. Well, we called him the Monday Morning Killer because he always struck on Monday mornings. You know, when people were getting ready to go to work or school when their guard was down because they never thought anything like that would happen at that time of day. At night after dark, yes, or when walking home alone, but never at a time as innocent as a Monday morning. He struck fear into the entire community. The guy was never caught. He just stopped killing or maybe moved on."

I leaned back in my chair and drummed my pencil on the table. "But that was back in the seventies?" I said. "More than forty years ago? Could it be the same guy?"

Mike shrugged. "Serial Killers have been known to have dormant periods. You're the expert. You know more about that than I do. You have a degree in this stuff, right?"

I nodded. "I do. But I don't think I ever heard of anyone taking a forty-year cool down."

"Maybe he didn't cool down; maybe he continued killing somewhere else, maybe using other methods," Weasel suggested.

"There would still be similarities," I said, "in his MO."

"Maybe he was in prison," Weasel said. "For something else. Violence against a girlfriend, something like that."

I nodded. It was plausible. "That's one explanation. It could also be a copycat, someone imitating his MO. He was, after all, quite famous around here, I am assuming?"

Mike nodded. "He was on everybody's lips."

I exhaled and looked at my colleagues.

"What can be a monster to most, can end up being a hero to some," I said. "The few that dream of repeating his atrocities, of becoming famous themselves." I looked at Weasel. "You might need to buckle up. It won't take the press long to add the numbers and get the same result we have here. You're in for a storm."

CHAPTER THIRTY-NINE

August 2018

Diane was still in awe. She could hardly believe what Jack had done for her. At first, when he had arrived with all the furniture, she felt inclined to tell him she didn't want it. She was afraid of what he might think, that if she accepted this gift, he would think she wanted more. She knew he was married, but according to his mother, it wasn't happily. Shannon was away too much and left him all alone with the responsibilities. How much of it was his mother's interpretations, Diane didn't know, but she really didn't want to come in the middle of anything. She had no time for any more drama in her life, as she'd had her share of it the past several years.

But then Jack had shown her all the nice furniture, and she couldn't say no. Of course, she couldn't. She desperately needed it, and if God answers your prayer, you better accept it, right? Diane had been praying for new furniture and so what if God chose Jack to be His messenger?

Now, as she was heading home after working at the motel all day, she felt a sense of relief go through her body. The sun felt nice on her face as she got out of the car, even though she was sweating heavily in the heat. In her purse, she had her paycheck that she would cash tomorrow. Her very first paycheck, and even though it wasn't much, it was definitely a start. She was making a little money now and felt like her life was finally beginning. Things were finally shaping up.

I knew you'd come through for me, God. I knew you would. It doesn't happen the way I want it to, or the way I expect it to, but you always come through for me.

Diane smiled at Mr. Fogerty as she walked up to her house. He was standing on his porch, as usual. He sent her a glare that gave her the chills, and she hurried up onto her own porch.

What was he doing out there all the time anyway? He just stood there, all the time. It felt like he was watching her. Even at nighttime when she came out to have her one-a-day cigarette on the porch, he would be there, looking at her in that odd fashion. It always gave her the chills. She didn't know why. Maybe it was just because he never spoke to her; maybe it was because he was just always there.

Diane approached her door and found the keys in her purse while listening to Tim and Tiffany going at it as always. The yelling was becoming a nuisance, especially when it happened at nighttime and they would keep her up, but somehow it was also a little comforting. On some days when she felt lonely, it felt good to know that they were there, right next door, even if they were fighting. As she found the keys, the yelling turned to kissing, and she could see them through the window going at it, him lifting her up against the wall. She moved her eyes as the loud moaning took over. They did that a lot too. After the yelling that was.

Diane didn't envy them one bit. She was happy just to have herself to deal with these days. And Misty of course.

"Misty?" she yelled as she opened the door. "I'm home."

Diane walked inside and put her purse down, then walked through the living room looking for the cat. It was usually happy to greet her when she came home.

"Misty? Where are you?"

That's odd.

Diane walked to the kitchen where the cat's water bowl and food were left untouched. Her heart sank as she looked around her.

All the cabinet doors were open. Every freakin' cabinet in the entire kitchen.

Diane backed up, holding a hand to her pounding chest. And that was when she saw that she had been wrong. Not all the cabinet doors were open. There was one that was still closed and, from behind it, she could hear a meowing. Diane rushed to it and opened the door, and the cat sprang out into her arms, making an awful noise.

Diane stood for a long time and stared at the kitchen, her hands holding the cat, shaking heavily. All the gaping cabinets stared back at her like they were laughing.

Diane regained her calmness, then rushed to them and closed them all one by one.

CHAPTER FORTY

I like to toy with them. Is it wrong? Yes, but hey, that's me. Everything I do is sick.

As I got more and more comfortable with my killings, I started to play with them before I struck, during my stalking phase. I even made the phase last longer and longer and toyed with the idea of letting them know that someone was stalking them. Why? Because I wanted them to fear me; I wanted to see that fear in their face when they received the flowers, when they came home, and I had been lying in their bed even though they knew they had made it that same morning. I loved seeing their faces as they realized I had access to their house at any time I wished. And I liked the thought that I could strike at any time I desired. Sometimes, I would hide in my future victims' houses for hours and just watch them from inside a closet or standing behind a door, and they wouldn't even know

I was there. Then as they went to bed, I would stare at them in the darkness, watching them sleep. I liked knowing that I had their lives in my full mercy. I was the one who'd decide if they lived or died. And I wanted them to know that. I had complete power over them.

The police, on the other hand, had no idea. I mean, they would come close sometimes. At one point, they raided a house across the street from me and arrested the guy who lived there. Of course, I thought they came for me when I saw them drive onto the street. I was certain of it, but to my surprise, they stopped across the street instead, and I watched them storm the house and grab the guy. As you can imagine, that was tremendously amusing to me. I even went so far as to walk out there and talk to one of the officers who was guarding, asking him what was happening. He said he couldn't tell me anything, but then I kept asking, was it the Monday Morning Killer? Then he nodded; can you imagine? He said they believed so. I felt such a thrill in the pit of my stomach that I almost laughed out loud, but of course, I kept my calm and told him that I appreciated his service and that it was good to know this killer was finally caught, so the rest of us law-abiding citizens could sleep well at night again.

And he bought into it. Every part of my little act. He even ended our conversation by telling me he was happy to help.

The scene was so obscure and yet so thrilling I had to do

it again. I found out where the detectives working the case usually hung out after work and then one day I walked in there and bought them a beer, telling them I wanted to thank them for all they did to catch this bastard.

And they talked to me. I asked them about the investigation, and they told me where they were at, how much they had and everything. It was such an amazing thrill, almost bigger than the killing itself, that I kept returning there at least once a week, while keeping track of the investigation, getting a picture of how much they knew and where they were at. And to my surprise, they were nowhere near finding me. At one point, one of the detectives even told me they appreciated observant and caring citizens like me. It made it all worth it to know that they had the backup from people, that people cared what they did. I bought him another beer just for that remark alone, and we drank it, and they had no idea. I know they considered me a nuisance, but nuisances aren't killers. I got in their way, yes. But friendly nuisances are dismissed. I was proud of myself for not losing it at that point, for keeping my composure. It is hard when you live a double life, when there are two realities. It's enough to drive most men mad.

Except me. I could take it. I could continue for the rest of my life.

CHAPTER FORTY-ONE

August 2018

"You were on fire last night."

Jack sounded excited on the phone. Shannon had called him an hour before tonight's show to hear his voice.

"I just watched a piece on TV about you and about the concert," he said. "They said you're better than ever."

Shannon smiled. It felt good to talk to him again. She had been upset about the fact that he had given all that furniture to that Diane woman he used to date, but now it was like it didn't matter so much anymore. Shannon felt so much better, and she didn't really want to be mad at Jack. She wanted to be happy and dance and sing. Boy, how she wanted to sing.

"It was really good. I had tons of fun."

"How are you?" he asked.

"Great! Never better," she said, almost laughing. It was the truth. She couldn't remember feeling this good since before she had Angela. She felt so strong and like she had the energy of her twenty-year-old self. Like she used to be.

"That's awesome, Shannon," he said. "You're greatly missed, though. Tyler has been crying a lot today. He says he misses you."

"Oh, poor baby," she said. "He'll be fine, though."

Jack went quiet on the other end. "Are you sure you're okay?" he said after a little pause.

"I told you. I'm great. Like the tiger in the cereal commercial," she said and laughed. "GRRREAT!"

Another silence and Shannon looked at her makeup in the mirror. Her vision was a little blurry, so she blinked a couple of times till her face finally cleared. She even looked great. And best of all, her hand wasn't hurting at all. Not even one little eensy teensy bit.

Eensy teensy bit? Was that even a saying? It should be, she thought to herself. It really should.

"Are you sure you're okay?" Jack asked again.

Shannon turned away from the mirror. "Yes, Jack. You've asked me that three times. I'm fine. Really. I'm just very, very happy; that's all."

"That's…great," Jack said. "Listen…I have an issue with the twins. I have to go. Talk to you later. Have a wonderful concert."

"Oh, I will," Shannon said. "It'll be the best one yet."

They hung up, and Shannon put the phone down. She stared at it on the make-up counter in front of her, wondering if Jack had always been so boring. It was almost depressing to talk to him. He had kind of gotten her a little down, and that wasn't good right before a concert. Maybe she shouldn't call him so close to her concerts anymore. He used to make her feel good about herself, but today it seemed to have the opposite effect.

There was a light knock on the door, and her manager peeked inside. Shannon smiled blissfully.

"You ready to knock them out of the park once again?"

Shannon giggled. "Never been more ready in my life."

CHAPTER FORTY-TWO

August 2018

She was sitting in her kitchen, staring at the cabinets, drumming her fingers impatiently on the table that Jack had given her. Misty had lost interest in her and what she was doing long ago and was now strolling happily around like nothing had happened. Diane, on the other hand, couldn't find rest. Ever since Jean had told her what happened in her house, she had found it hard to find peace there.

She had even been stupid enough to research the murder. Online, she had found old articles with pictures from the scene, and it had made her even more uneasy when staying in the house alone.

Diane turned her head and looked at the floor.

She had removed the wooden floors, and she could no longer see the blood, but that didn't matter. She still knew it was there; she knew that was where the father of the family had been murdered. It was the police's theory that he had been fighting the killer as he entered the house, that the dad had tried to protect his family, and that was why there had been so much blood. The killer had cut him with a knife, according to the autopsy report. He had bruises that signaled he had fought for his life. And for the lives of his loved ones.

Diane shuddered and looked away. Her eyes fell on the back door leading to the yard. The killer had come through that door when he entered. He had surprised the mother, who was in the middle of making lunches for her children before school.

Diane imagined her standing in her kitchen, making peanut butter sandwiches, then yelling at the kids that it was soon time to go. Had the kids been upstairs when the killer entered? They didn't know, but they were found up there, plastic bags wrapped around their small necks. Both the mom and dad were found up in their bedroom too. Staged, according to the police. Like they were on display. They didn't know for sure if the mother had been killed upstairs or in the kitchen before she was dragged up there along with her dead husband. Diane looked at the stairs where she had seen the blood. She could almost hear the father's head slam against the steps as he was dragged up there. Was he already dead or did he die upstairs? No one knew. Only the killer himself knew, and he was never caught.

The Monday Morning Killer, they had named him.

What a silly name.

Silly as it might be, it still brought goosebumps to Diane's neck, and she rose to her feet. She walked to the cabinet and grabbed herself a glass, then poured some water from the fridge and drank some. She looked at the cabinet door and wondered who in their right mind would lock her cat inside one of these cabinets.

Diane had a pretty good idea who it might be.

She emptied the glass, then walked toward the living room with the intention of going to bed, when the lights in her house suddenly went out. Diane let out a small scream as she realized she was now in total darkness. She ran to the counter and grabbed a knife from the block. With it firmly grasped in her hand, she looked around, reacting to a movement she detected coming from the living room.

She waited, panting and sweating for a few seconds till the movement approached her, then as she got ready to jump forward, she realized it was just her cat.

It was just Misty.

"Silly cat."

Diane bent down and grabbed the cat in her arm when she thought she heard another sound, like someone bigger coming toward her. She screamed loudly and held out the knife in front of her.

"W-who is there?"

Diane took a step forward when there was another sound. She gasped and looked to the side but couldn't see anything. Then she turned and looked to her left when she thought she spotted someone. Diane shrieked, then stormed for the back door. She slammed it open and ran into the yard, panting and without looking where she was going.

She ran straight into someone.

"Hey, hey, hey," the voice said. He grabbed her by the shoulders. "Diane, what's going on?"

Panting, Diane looked up, and in the light from his flashlight, she could see Dennis's face.

"Are you okay?" he asked. "You look awful."

Diane gazed back toward her house, then up at him again. "I…I thought, th-there was someone… the lights went out…w-what are you doing in my yard?"

"I was just…wait…you don't think that…I…? Oh, that's rich. No. I was just over here to check on the power lines. They run through your yard, see?" he said and shone his flashlight at them. "One of them came down. That's what caused the power outage on the entire street. You thought I was…that I would…"

She shook her head. "No, no, of course not."

"The lights went out in all the houses in the street," he said. "That's why I came into your yard. A power line went down in your yard and caused it. I'm going back to call FPL now."

"I…I…Okay. So, it wasn't just my house?"

Dennis shook his head. "No, silly. Paranoid much, are we?"

Diane chuckled. "Yeah, well. When you live alone, sometimes your imagination can run away with you, right?"

He nodded with a skeptical look. "Right. Well,

I'll get back and call them. Camille and the kids are playing hide and go seek with flashlights. They love the stuff. Say, are you going to be all right?"

She nodded.

Dennis smiled. "All right. Let me know if you're not. I'm right across the street, okay?"

"O-okay."

"You don't have a flashlight in your house?" he asked just as he was about to leave.

She shook her head. "No."

"Here. Have mine. You're in Florida now. You need a flashlight. Power outages are almost an everyday thing during thunderstorm season. Not to mention when the hurricanes come. You've got to stay prepared in these parts. Prepared for *anything* to happen."

He said the last part with a wink and Diane took the flashlight, her hands still shaking.

Dennis then turned around and walked out of her yard. Watching him leave, Diane found her cell phone in her pocket and dialed a number that she had sworn she wasn't going to dial again.

CHAPTER FORTY-THREE

August 2018

"Tyler is such a pain in the a…"

I raised my finger in front of Abigail. "Don't you dare finish that sentence."

Next to her, her brother closed his eyes and I knew he was wishing she would. He loved it when Abigail got herself in trouble and often would do anything he could to make her. Meanwhile, he had that innocent act going on, but I was on to him.

Abigail stopped. "But he is. He took my favorite slime and poured it in the toilet. It was my favorite, Dad."

"He's a kid, Abigail. He doesn't know what he's doing half the time. Can't you just make something new?"

She looked disappointed. "I could, but…"

"But what?"

"Colin made it for me."

"Colin?" I asked.

"Yes, Colin. The kid who lives next door," Abigail said, annoyed that I didn't know who he was. "Don't you ever keep up?"

"I'm sorry I don't know who Colin is," I said, "but in case you haven't noticed, I've been quite busy around here."

"He's Abigail's *bo-o-yfriend*," Austin said, mocking her.

"He's not."

"He so is."

"Is not."

"Okay, stop," I finally broke in. If I didn't stop them, they could go on like that for hours, and I was—to be perfectly honest—completely worn out. I was done listening to the kids argue.

"Go get ready for bed," I told them.

"But, *Daaa-a-d*, we still have half an hour. We never go to bed till nine o'clock."

I bent over and looked my daughter in the eye. "Make an exception."

"Ah, man," she said and walked off, shoulders slumped.

The two other A's followed her up the stairs. Meanwhile, I picked up seven different toys that Tyler had placed in strange places. I had put Tyler down right before his sister had discovered the slime in the toilet, luckily. Otherwise, I wasn't sure he would still be alive. It always amazed me how great a difference there was between my own kids and the children I met in my line of work. I often wanted to tell my kids about them, teach them to be more grateful, but I also had to realize I couldn't blame them for being normal, for not knowing the evil that lurked out there, for not knowing that their life could change forever in less than a second. That was, after all, the difference between being a child and an adult. The belief that nothing bad could ever hit you. It was an innocence I wanted my kids to keep. An innocence I so often saw being ripped out of children when meeting them at work.

I threw Tyler's toys in the basket in the living room and closed the lid. I stared out at the ocean. It was so dark out there, and I couldn't even see the beach. I sighed and missed Shannon more than ever. I kept worrying about her, especially after I had spoken to her earlier. She had sounded so off. Something was wrong, but I couldn't put my finger on it. She wasn't herself; that was for sure. I was wondering if this tour was getting to her, if it was becoming too much.

I didn't get to finish the thought before my phone rang. It was Diane. She spoke without breathing.

"Jack. It's Diane. I had promised myself I wouldn't call, and I was certain I wouldn't because I didn't want you to think that I, I mean I don't, I really don't, but I think I might…"

"Diane, calm down," I said. "You're not making much sense here. What's going on?"

There was a pause, and I realized she was crying on the other end.

"Diane?"

"I'm scared, Jack. I'm so scared."

CHAPTER FORTY-FOUR

August 2018

"I'm so sorry to call you out here like this. I really am. Dragging you away from your kids and everything."

Diane showed me inside her beach house and locked the door behind me. She stared at me with almost mad eyes.

I grabbed a chair and sat down in her kitchen.

"That's okay, Diane, my mom came over to put them to bed. She'll stay with them till I get back. What's going on? You said you were scared?"

She sat down across from me. I could see her hands trembling when she bit her nails.

"What's going on, Diane?" I asked.

"It's this house," she said, shaking her head. "It's

driving me crazy."

"Take it from the beginning, would you?"

"You know the blood, right? On the floors?"

"Yes, you showed me."

"There *was* someone killed here," she said. "An entire family. Father, mother, and two children. Massacred in this house. Right over there. That's where the dad was killed, murdered."

I nodded. "I know, Diane. I've recently…come across this news as well. They called him the Monday Morning Killer. He raged this town back in the seventies and eighties. But no one has heard from him since. His last killing—that we know of was in nineteen-eighty-four, ten years after he began, he suddenly stopped. No one knows what happened to him then. He might have died in a car accident or gotten himself killed somehow. He might also have been in jail, or maybe he just stopped. It's been known to happen."

"And the new killings?" she asked. "Is that him too? Has he come back?"

I shrugged. "He could have. Might have resurfaced somehow. Or maybe someone is copying him. We don't know yet. It's been known to happen. You know, in sort of a weird way to honor him."

Diane swallowed. "Should I be afraid?"

"I can't see why you would be more scared than anyone else."

"Because I live in the house where he killed his first victims?" she asked.

"He has no history of returning to his crime scenes, so I don't think there is any need to be afraid of that," I said, trying to sound as reassuring as I was capable. Fact was, I was nervous for her since I feared that the fact that she had moved into this particular house was the reason why this killer had resurfaced. But I didn't want to frighten her. There was no reason why this killer should return to this house.

Unless he wants to relive his first thrill.

"I'm sure you'll be fine," I said. "Now, tell me what scared you so much tonight?"

She stared at me for a few seconds. "Today, when I came back home, all the cabinet doors in my kitchen were open, except one. Inside that one, I found my cat. Later on, all the lights went out. My neighbor said it was a power outage."

I leaned back in my chair.

"It scared me, Jack."

"All the cabinets were open? And you're certain you didn't leave them that way when you left and just forgot about it?"

She looked at me like I was an idiot. She had lit a bunch of candles everywhere, and I was slightly nervous she might end up burning the entire house down, but she had told me she needed there to be as much light as possible till FPL managed to get the power back on.

"And leave my cat inside one of them so he couldn't get out and eat? How crazy do you think I am?" Diane asked.

"Of course not. I don't think you're crazy at all, just making sure. And the power?"

"I met my neighbor Dennis in my yard."

I wrinkled my forehead. "What was he doing in your yard?"

"He said the power line fell in my yard and caused the power outage."

"And this happened right after the lights went out? You ran into your yard? How did he know so quickly that the problem was in your yard?" I asked. "It could have been anywhere in the street?"

"That's what I want to know," she said.

"Sounds a little off to me," I said. "Can I take a look at that power line?"

"Sure," she said and stood up. She grabbed a flashlight and turned it on. "I'll show you."

CHAPTER FORTY-FIVE

August 2018

"It's been cut."

I looked at Diane and shined the light at the dangling power line so she could see for herself.

"With a knife," I said. "This was no accident. There's even a ladder over there, see?"

"That's my ladder," she said. "Or…it belongs to the house. It was in the shed when I moved in."

"I see," I said and shone the light around me to see if I could find any traces or even a footprint in the grass, but there was nothing. It had been unusually dry for the season, and we hadn't had any thunderstorms for at least a week.

Diane looked at me. She grabbed my arm. "I'm scared, Jack."

I nodded. "I understand, but…"

She shook her head. "Not of him. I mean, yes, I'm scared of the killer too, but I think it might be someone else who did these things."

I stared at her. "What do you mean?"

"I haven't really told you why I moved here, have I?" she asked rhetorically. "I haven't told anyone."

"I'm listening."

"I have sort of…run away. I mean, I'm trying to get a divorce; I will eventually, but I just couldn't… he just wouldn't…he wouldn't stop, you know?"

"I'm assuming you're talking about your ex-husband?" I said, sensing a piece of the puzzle falling into place.

"Yes. He was…"

"Abusive?"

She nodded her head. "Not in a physical way. It was more in that he dominated me and told me what to do and when to do it and, little by little, isolated me from the world and the people who loved me. Once I realized what he was doing, it was too late. He controlled every little detail of my life like when I woke up in the morning, what I wore to work, who I spoke to, what I ate for lunch and with whom. He even controlled when I showered. I can't tell you when it all started; it sort of snuck up on me. I wanted to please him; I wanted to keep him happy, and soon I had completely lost myself."

"But you finally got away?" I asked.

She nodded. "I left without a word. One day when he came home from work, I simply wasn't there. I had packed my things during the day instead of going to work and, when he called to check in on me, I pretended I was still at work. Usually, he would stop by the shop to check in on me during the day, so I had picked a day when he was in meetings all day, so I knew he couldn't do that. It was all very carefully planned. Yet, once he found the note and realized I had left, he began his search. It didn't take him long to track me down, by calling around and threatening people that he was going to kill himself. I had only told one friend where I went, and she cracked when he told her he would hang himself. Soon, the guy was at my doorstep at the condo I had rented, screaming and yelling at me to open the door. When I finally caved because I didn't want the neighbors to be bothered, he was bleeding out of his mouth and was all pathetic, crying, telling me he had an ulcer and that it had erupted. I got so scared when I saw all the blood that I immediately let him inside and tried to help him. He told me he was going to die and if I didn't come back, he would kill himself. He would drive the car into the harbor with himself in it. I spoke later to a friend who is a doctor, and she told me you only bleed like that if you bite your own tongue. He bit himself so hard, just to get me back. I was scared he would harm himself."

"And, of course, you couldn't live with that guilt, so you went back?" I asked, knowing this type of story a little too well.

She nodded. "And once I did, everything was oh so wonderful in the beginning, but soon it turned worse. I couldn't do anything without him being terrified I was going to leave him again. I wasn't even allowed to talk on the phone with my friends or my mother. If I did, he would assume I was about to plan another escape. As soon as he felt safe that I was back to stay, he began yelling at me night after night for what I had done and the pain I had caused him. Everything was my fault. In the end, I just couldn't stand his abuse anymore, and I began to fear him. His mental stability was spiraling downward fast, and I began fearing for my life. I thought maybe he would kill me while I was asleep or maybe burn the house down with the both of us in it. Stuff like that. He even said some things as a joke from time to time. Things like, at least if we died now, we'd go together. Or that he believed Romeo and Juliet was a great story, especially how they died together. I would fear for my life when driving with him because he could say stuff for fun like, 'What if I just kept going till we hit that wall over there?' or he would run a red light, grinning and yelling at me, 'What are you scared of?' Stuff like that scared me senseless. And I started to plan my second escape. This time, I didn't tell a soul. I just left. I didn't even pack much since I had to do it fast and get as far away as possible. I had never told him about you and so when I saw your post on Facebook about this new town you had moved to a few years ago, and you wrote that your parents lived here as well, running the old motel, I realized that's where I should go. Your family has always been so good to me, when I had troubles at home with my dad. I could always come to your house. Your mom would take care of me and give me a bed for the night if I needed or just lend me an ear if I needed to talk. It's something you never forget, when someone shows you love like that. I have never forgotten you or your family. Sometimes, I even wonder how my life would have turned out if we hadn't broken up. If we had..."

Diane lifted her eyes in the darkness and looked at me. They sparkled in the light of her flashlight. I swallowed hard, remembering how madly in love with her I had been back then. She was the one who had broken up with me because she needed to be a free spirit when taking on the world, she had said back then. She had been so full of life, so ready to conquer the world. But I guess the world had chewed her up and spit her back out like it had with most of us. Life hadn't really turned out to be what we thought it would. I had a pretty decent one; I had it better than her, but still. Things had been tough. Still were.

I swallowed as our eyes locked. Emotions so deep and so well-buried were threatening to resurface and make themselves relevant again.

But I couldn't let them.

Diane leaned over, and I wondered what it would be like to kiss her again. For one unforgivable moment, I looked at those red lips and wanted to taste them again.

Yet, I didn't. Instead, I pulled away with a deep sigh and so did she.

"I'm sorry," she said.

"No…no…I'm just…I need to get back to the kids."

She nodded. "Of course. Don't worry about me. I'll be fine."

I started to walk backward out of the yard, my heart pounding in my chest.

"I'll check in on you in the morning, okay? Call me if anything happens. I'll send a patrol if you get scared, okay?"

She nodded. "O-okay."

I turned around and walked faster out of the yard and closed the gate in the fence behind me. With a deep sigh, I closed my eyes and cursed myself for letting it get this far.

As I opened them again and started to walk back toward the Jeep, I spotted an older man standing on the porch at the neighbor's house. It wasn't so much the fact that he was standing there that made me wonder; it was the way his eyes followed my every move like he was sizing me up.

I shook the thought and hurried to my car, then drove off, reminding myself to call Shannon and say goodnight before I went to bed.

PART THREE

CHAPTER FORTY-SIX

Cocoa Beach 2011

The boy ran home from school. As soon as the bus had let him off, he stormed down the street toward his house. He rushed past the neighbors' houses and didn't even have time to say hello to Mrs. Johnson's dog like he usually did. The boy ran to the door, slammed it open, and rushed inside. He looked first in the kitchen, then the living room, and finally the garage.

But his dad wasn't there.

Maybe he'll come back before you go to bed?

Every day since his father had left, slamming the door, the boy had been praying and hoping that he would come back, that he would be there once he came back from school. But, so far, he hadn't.

And it had been more than two weeks now. His father had never stayed away this long. He always came back. He always did.

When finding only his mother and baby sister inside the house, the boy hurried into the yard to be with his chickens. He opened the enclosure and walked in, then closed it behind him. He sat on the ground, then began to cry, hiding his face in his arms.

Victoria came to him and picked at his shoe.

"Why isn't he coming back?" he asked.

Naturally, the chicken's only answer was a cluck. It made the boy chuckle. Few things in this world could cheer the boy up like the chickens could. After his dad had left, they were all he had.

The boy turned his head and stared at the house. He could see his mother through the window. He narrowed his eyes and felt such rage stir up inside of him.

"She's the reason he's not coming back, isn't she?" he asked the chickens, who still just clucked and staggered around, finding food.

The boy stared at his mother while the anger rose inside of him, when his sister came out on the porch and yelled at him, telling him he had to come inside.

The boy rose to his feet, told his chickens he was going to come back soon, then rushed toward the back porch and ran inside. He walked into the kitchen where his mother stood. She was waiting for him.

He bowed his head when he saw the anger in her eyes. She had been even meaner to him than usual since his dad had left. It was like when she didn't have his dad to yell at, then she yelled at the boy instead. And it seemed like she was just looking for things to yell at him about. It could be anything and everything. There really wasn't any indication as to what would set her off.

"What's that?" she asked now.

She pointed at his shoes.

"Is that bird poop? Were you in with those disgusting birds again?"

"I'll wipe it off," he said. "Don't worry."

"Oh, you don't get to tell me when to worry, do you hear me?" she asked.

He avoided her eyes and stared at the floor. "O-of course not."

The boy had awoken the rage of the beast; he knew it very well, and he also knew there wasn't anything he could do at this point. Once she reached this level, there was no turning back.

His mother reached out, grabbed his head, and slammed it against the wall next to them.

"And who do you think is going to clean up this mess, huh? Who is going to clean up after your mess, huh?" she said as she banged his head against the wall, again and again, yelling at him.

"You're just as useless as your dad was."

BAM, she slammed it again.

"All men are. Useless."

BAM.

"Useless."

BAM

"And then they just take off and leave."

BAM.

"You're just like him, do you know that? All men are the same. ALL of them."

BAM. BAM.

"I wish I never had you. I wish I never had a disgusting boy like you who will grow up to be a disgusting man like your father!"

BAM. BAM. BAM.

On and on she continued until the boy heard a ringing in his ears and tasted blood in his mouth. When she saw the blood, she finally let him go, and he sank to the floor where she let him stay till he was able to get up on his own.

CHAPTER FORTY-SEVEN

August 2018

"I just don't understand why I can't find him."

I exhaled and leaned back in my chair. Several days had passed, and my investigation had completely stalled. The media was all over the story of the Monday Morning Killer's return, and Weasel had her work cut out for her, trying to keep people calm and keeping the panic at bay.

Meanwhile, I had tried to get ahold of Steve Carver, the kid who had survived the Monday Morning Killer's first kill. Mike was sitting on the other side of my desk, behind my many piles of old newspaper articles and files from the archive. I had studied everything that had ever been written about the Monday Morning Killer and his victims and still I was no closer to who he really was.

Mike sipped his coffee then put the cup down in a rare empty spot on my desk.

"What can I tell you?" he said. "People aren't always that easy to find. Maybe he wanted to disappear."

I grabbed the old file with the boy's testimony from back in seventy-four. He was seventeen at the time of the killings. I had read it over and over again, every little detail of how he came home from school, holding the envelope to his chest, the envelope containing the letter about his scholarship that he was looking forward to handing to his parents because they would be so proud of him. He had seen the dog in the neighbor's yard and went to grab it; then when he came inside, he realized something was wrong when he spotted the half made peanut butter sandwich on the counter. The rest of the testimony was so terrifying I didn't like to even think about it. Finding your parents like that and then your siblings was one thing, but then to realize that the killer was still in the house and run for your life. Even being grabbed and beaten by him before getting away and then hiding underneath a dock till sunset in the murky water with the threat of alligators. It was inhumane. No one knew what that would do to a young kid. I wanted desperately to talk to him about what he remembered from back then. He had to be in his late fifties by now, but a thing like this wasn't easy to forget even if you wanted to. There had to be at least something that he could tell me to help me find this guy. Something they hadn't thought about asking him back then. If it was, in fact, the same guy we were looking for and not someone copying him. It tortured me that they had never found him back then. All they knew was that his mother's car was stolen from the garage and left in a ditch in the mainland. But the kid had to have looked into the eyes of the madman. He had to have seen him. There had to be something he could tell me to help me.

"What do you mean?" I asked.

"Well, he did become sort of a celebrity around here," Mike continued. "All the newspapers and TV Stations ran interviews with the kid who lived. He might have moved away to get away from the press. It's not very likely that he stayed around here with all those memories. He probably needed a brand-new start somewhere else."

I sighed, knowing Mike was probably right. I

had put out a request nationally with our colleagues, in case his name rang a bell somewhere, but those things took forever, and I wasn't sure of any response since it wasn't an urgent matter.

I looked at the picture of the young boy from the police file. His terrified eyes stared back at me.

"There is one thing that bothers me," I said.

Mike sipped his coffee with a smirk. "Only one, huh?"

"Well multiple, but this is one of them. The first time he killed, he let someone live. The same happened recently in the case of the Reynolds family. But not in any of the other cases. No one has ever survived him since."

"Maybe it's a way of marking the fact that he is starting out? To let us know that the killings have begun and that it is him? How else would we know that he wears the same mask? Stuff like that gets those types going; you know that."

I nodded. "True. But there's another thing. The mother," I said and pulled out the Reynolds file.

"What about her?" he asked.

"She was decapitated in the Reynolds case. Not in the Carver case, not in the Carpenter case, or in any of the rest of them. Eight cases in total are what we have on him from the seventies and eighties. Eight families killed and destroyed. And now, two in two-thousand and eighteen. He takes some darn long breaks in between."

"Because he's clever," Mike said. "He knows to cool down when the ground is burning."

"But why change your MO if you're trying to get our attention?" I asked. "Why suddenly cut the head off the mother? All the others he killed with plastic bags."

"Except the Carver dad," Mike said. "He was strangled with a belt."

I nodded. "Right. Argh, it makes no sense."

Mike looked at his nails, then back at me. "Do you think that your little friend moving into the house triggered him to resurface?" he asked.

"That's one of my fears, yes," I said.

"What's another?" Mike asked.

"That he'll kill again before we stop him. Right now, I have nothing. The killer could be anyone for all I care. I don't even know his age in case it's a copycat we're looking for."

"It's not," Mike said and leaned forward.

"What? How can you be so sure?" I asked.

"The flowers," he said.

"What flowers?"

"Someone sent Steve's mother daisies about a

week before he killed her. Same thing happened to the next family he destroyed a few years later. Same thing happened to Mrs. Reynolds, and I'm pretty sure I saw a bouquet of daisies on the counter in Mrs. Carpenter's kitchen. This was never in any papers, and no one ever took any notice of it, except for me I guess. When the Monday Morning Killer reached his family number three, I was in the force and among the first responders. I remember telling my boss back then about it, but no one ever followed that lead or even contacted the florist that they came from, so I did, but it didn't lead anywhere. The flowers were paid for in cash, and no one remembered what the buyer looked like, except that he was tall. Later on, this was forgotten. But, the fact was, no newspapers ever mentioned it, and there is no way any copycat killer could know this part."

I leaned back in my chair, a sense of dread beginning to grow deep in my stomach.

"Daisies, huh?"

Mike nodded. "Daisies."

CHAPTER FORTY-EIGHT

August 2018

Shannon felt like dancing. She was done with her concert for today and staggered into her dressing room, still feeling so incredibly energized, even though she had just blown them out of the park for several hours.

"Whoo-hoo, way to go, Shannon!" Bruce exclaimed as he entered right behind her. "You were on fire tonight, girl. I am tellin' ya' they love you out there. Everyone does, especially the critics. You're getting rave reviews for this one as well."

Shannon sighed contentedly and put the guitar down. She moved her wrist back and forth with relief.

"Does it hurt?" Sarah asked as she came into

the dressing room as well and saw Shannon looking at her hand. Shannon lifted her head and looked at her assistant.

"Not even one bit. Can you believe it?"

Sarah bit her lip. Her eyes had that concerned look to them again, and it annoyed Shannon.

"That's amazing, Shan," Bruce said indifferently. He was already on his phone, walking away while talking to someone else.

"Don't you want to sit down?" Sarah said. "Have a little break? You've been going at it nonstop for days now. Interview after interview, followed by concerts. You hardly eat and barely sleep. You must be exhausted."

"I'm fine, really," Shannon said and sat at the makeup table and started to remove the thick layer of concealer. This was her least favorite part of the night, taking off all the heavy make-up. She hated seeing that pale old face that was revealed behind it.

"Are you sure…?" Sarah asked. She glanced at the glass of pills on the counter, and Shannon saw her do it but ignored her.

"So, you have two days off now," she said. "Maybe you'll be able to get some rest?"

Shannon gasped happily. "That's right. I have two days off now. I completely forgot about that."

"I think it'll do us all some good," Sarah said and sat down with a tired sigh. "I, for one, want to do some shopping tomorrow. Maybe treat myself to a day of spa treatments. How about you?"

Shannon looked at Sarah in the mirror, then at her own reflection. She really didn't feel like resting. She didn't feel like going to a spa or shopping. She wanted to do something, something fun. She had all this energy and felt like she couldn't stop now, or she might burn out. She might lose the energy. She couldn't risk that.

"I think I'm gonna take some time off for myself too."

"And you're sure you don't need me? I mean, I can cancel my plans if you need me to stick around?" she asked.

"No. Of course not. Go have your spa day. I'll be fine on my own for once. It'll probably even be nice just to be by myself and relax. You're right. I need it."

Sarah sighed contently and leaned back in her chair. She gave Shannon one last concerned look, then seemed to let it go.

CHAPTER FORTY-NINE

August 2018

She had felt uneasy all day while working at the motel. She couldn't stop thinking about her ex, Frank, and wondering if he had really found her here. How was that even possible? No one knew where she was, not even her own mother, and she had stopped using any social media. All day long, she thought she saw him or looked over her shoulder because she felt like she was being watched. It was about to drive her nuts.

Diane had hardly closed an eye all night; she couldn't stop worrying about him being here and kept hearing noises in the house. All day yesterday, she had felt like someone was observing her and she couldn't shake the feeling that someone was. Come to think of it, she had felt that way ever since she moved into the house. Maybe Frank had been on her tail all along? Could he really be that vicious?

You know he can.

Diane shuddered at the mere thought of him. To think that he had touched her and slept with her night after night made her want to throw up. Everything about him made her shiver in disgust and contempt. Yet she feared him more than any serial killer.

Because he had nothing to lose anymore.

Diane got to her feet and stretched, thinking she'd better get ready for a new day. She took a shower, got dressed, and went into the kitchen when she spotted Dennis across the street, mowing his lawn, again. It was almost like a ritual with that man, wasn't it? Every freakin' day, he cut the grass like it wasn't allowed to grow even an inch above what he wanted it to be. His excuse was that it grew like crazy in the Florida heat. It seemed a little overindulgent to Diane. Like he was such perfectionistic that the grass had to be completely correct all the time.

It reminded her slightly of Frank. He too had paid too much attention to details, making her life miserable by constantly finding faults everywhere and especially with her. Everything had to be in line in the cabinets, the labels turned outwards. Every towel had to be folded the same way, and every shirt had to be ironed to perfection. It had started out being cute but then taken over her life completely. If she messed something up, like she missed one of the cat's hairballs when vacuuming, he would yell at her for days. It was exhausting to live with someone like that, and suddenly Diane felt such deep sympathy for Dennis's wife, Camille. Having two children with a man like that had to be tough.

Diane walked out to the driveway and picked up the paper. Dennis waved at her while sitting on his mower. His sweaty torso was glistening, yet every hair on his head was pointing in the right direction. She waved back and smiled. Then she looked at the street in front of her house when she realized something was missing.

Her car.

Diane stopped and looked at the empty spot in front of her house. Where was her car? She had driven home from work the night before and parked it where she usually did, right in front of her house. Why wasn't it there?

Diane felt confused and looked around when she suddenly spotted it. It was parked in front of

Mr. Fogerty's house. Diane had to rub her eyes to make sure she wasn't still asleep.

"What the…?"

Diane ran inside and found the keys to it inside her purse, then walked back out and stared at the car. Could she really have been that tired last night? It was very unlike her.

Diane shook her head and walked to the car and got inside. She put the key in the ignition, but the car just coughed and didn't start. Diane sighed and leaned back in her seat.

"Great. That's really great."

She got out and slammed the door, hard, when she spotted Mr. Fogerty standing on his porch, staring at her with those angry eyes of his.

"I'm sorry," she said. "I'll make sure it's moved…later."

With irritated steps, Diane went back into her house and slammed the door behind her. She looked at the clock. She'd have to take the bus to the motel today and then deal with the car later.

She stared at the purse on the kitchen counter, when she realized something. This wasn't where she had put it last night. She was certain she had put it on the dresser in her bedroom. What was it doing on the kitchen counter?

Diane shook the thought and walked up to her bedroom. She stood in the doorway and stared at her bed, her legs beginning to shake.

Someone had been lying in it. She distinctly remembered making it this morning when she got up. Now, there was an obvious imprint of a figure a lot taller and heavier than she was.

CHAPTER FIFTY

August 2018

Tyler complained that he had a scratchy throat, but I ended up sending him to the daycare center anyway. He had developed a tendency to try and get out of going recently—ever since Shannon went on tour—and I had a feeling this was one of those days where he just wanted to stay home. I couldn't blame him. After getting five kids ready for school and fighting with Emily about doing laundry or at least doing something instead of just becoming a hermit in her room, I was exhausted and wanted to take the day off myself. Just one day alone at the house, maybe go surfing for a little while. Just me. Alone. No demands, no crying, no fighting.

But I couldn't.

I had promised Parker, Josef, and Mark that I would find the guy who had killed their mothers and, in Parker's case, also his sister. I couldn't stop wondering about those two cases. Could it really be the same killer as it had been forty-four years ago? It had to be, right? Mike said so, with the flowers and everything.

While I was in the car on my way to the station, Diane called.

"Hi, Diane. What's up?" I asked, getting wind in my hair while driving with the top down as I usually did unless we had a thunderstorm.

"I think I'm going crazy."

I laughed. "You and me both, Diane."

"No, I'm serious. There is something seriously wrong here, and I think it's Frank. I think he found me. He's trying to drive me crazy."

"What happened?" I asked and turned into the parking lot behind the station. I nodded at the firefighters as they walked by. Their brand-new fire station was located right next to our old building, which also housed city hall.

"My car. I know I parked it outside my house last night and then this morning, it was parked in front of the neighbor's house."

"And you couldn't just have parked it in the wrong spot last night? You might have been tired?"

"I hardly think so. But I couldn't get it started. There is nothing new about that; it does that from time to time. But the thing is, my purse wasn't in its usual spot in my bedroom. It was in the kitchen, and that's where I keep my keys. Someone was in my house, Jack, I am not kidding you. Someone was in here while I slept and stole my purse with the keys to my car, then drove it to the neighbor's house and parked it there."

"But...why?" I asked.

"To drive me nuts. And get this. This morning when I came back from finding the car, someone had been lying in my bed. I know I made it when I got up. I always do, and the cover was still on it, but someone had been lying on it and made a huge imprint. I got so scared that I ran to the next-door neighbor's house and that's where I am now."

"That Dennis guy?"

"No, next door. Tim and Tiffany."

"The ones who fight a lot."

"Yes. He's not home, but she is. She told me I could stay as long as I wanted. But I have to go to work soon, so I think I'll just go to the bus and get to your parents' motel, then deal with this later on.

But, Jack, I am so scared. What if it is Frank? What if he's here to…Maybe I'm just being crazy. Maybe it's just the hormones."

She went silent.

"You're pregnant?" I asked.

She sighed deeply. "Yes."

"Does Frank know?"

She paused. "Yes. I told him a few days before I left. It was because of the pregnancy that I decided to leave the second time. I didn't want a child to grow up under those circumstances. I wanted a better future for my child."

"But now you're thinking that the fact that you're pregnant might make him even more determined to find you and bring you back. Or maybe even worse, kill you both for leaving him. I can't blame you."

"So, you think he did find me?" she asked. "I just don't understand how?"

"Psychopaths have their ways. I think it's mostly in that they don't ever give up. They're relentless. Maybe you should stay somewhere else tonight. I'm sure my parents can lend you a room at the motel for a few nights till we have this figured out."

"Okay," Diane said. "I'll talk to them when I get there."

"I'll have the patrol cars drive past your house a few times a day just to make sure no one is sneaking around in the area. Can you text me a picture of him, so they'll know who to look for?"

"O-of course. I'll do it right away. Listen, Jack. Thank you so much for taking me seriously. I don't think anyone else would have at this point. I am truly grateful for that."

"No problem, Diane. It's my job to keep you safe."

CHAPTER FIFTY-ONE

August 2018

Around lunchtime, I went to Juice N' Java to grab myself an Americano sandwich on sourdough, then took it with me back to the station and ate at my desk. I didn't really have time for a proper break, so I compromised.

I kept thinking about Diane and that ex-husband of hers. It seemed to be a bad case of harassment that he was exposing her to these days, and he sure sounded like a creep, but deep inside, something was nagging at me about it all. It was those silly flowers.

The daisies.

I ate my sandwich wondering about them and about what Mike had told me. He had been on the force for a long time. It was truly valuable to have his knowledge around, and I had to give it some extra thought.

I didn't want to tell Diane about it since there was no reason to scare her further, but I couldn't help wondering. Could it be a coincidence that Diane received daises when she moved into the very same house where the Monday Morning Killer had committed his first crime? Or could someone—like her ex-husband—be playing a cruel joke on her? Could it be a third person? Maybe a neighbor? Who else would know about the flowers? Mike had told me it wasn't mentioned anywhere since it had not been made public and that the detective who investigated the Monday Morning Killer back then hadn't believed it was important. I would give everything I had to have a chat with that detective, but unfortunately, he had died of cancer five years ago. All I had were his handwritten notes and the reports from back then. They had no computers, and everything was a mess, to be honest. Still, I went through each and every report once again, desperately searching for something to help me, anything that would stand out.

About an hour later, Joe Hall came to my desk and handed me a cup of coffee.

"Thought you needed it," he said.

I looked up and smiled. I grabbed the coffee and sipped it. "Thank you. I really did."

"So, what're you working at?"

"I'm just going through the old cases again."

"Finding anything interesting?" he asked and sipped his cup.

"Not really. It's so odd…" I grabbed my cup and sipped it again while staring out the window quickly, before returning to the report.

"What's odd?" Joe asked.

I looked at him, then shook my head. "Daisies."

"What do you mean daisies?"

I shook my head again. "It's probably nothing. How's the kid? How's Parker? You were out there earlier, right?"

Joe nodded. "Took the first shift before Marty took over."

"How is he?"

"Pretty good," he said. "The dad has been there almost every day. He's being discharged soon, they say. Jim Reynolds has said Parker can come live with him in Vero Beach. He's gonna need a lot of training to be able to walk normally, but they have great hopes for him they say."

"Maybe I should pay him another visit soon. He

must have seen more than he wants to tell me. I know he keeps stating that he doesn't remember anything, but I can't help feeling like he's just saying that. If he's doing better, then there's no harm in questioning him."

"Maybe go through the dad," Joe said. "He seems to have a good connection with the boy. It looks like the boy looks up to him a lot."

I nodded while biting my lip. "I think you might be right," I said and lifted my cup in recognition. "If I can get Jim to tell him to open up to me, then maybe he will. Good call."

I barely got to swallow the sip of my coffee before my phone rang. It was the daycare center. Tyler was running a fever again.

CHAPTER FIFTY-TWO

Cocoa Beach 2013

After his dad left, life became a living hell for the boy. His mother told him he was a plague, that all men were, and that he was never ever to get close to his sister or her again. She told him she didn't want him inside the house anymore and made him live in the shed in the backyard, where there was no AC and no toilets and when he asked to come inside and use the restroom, she told him to go in the yard. Showers he could take by using the hose, and she would put food for him on the doorstep of the shed. But under no circumstances was he ever allowed inside the house again. And if she caught him as much as staring at his sister, she would throw him into the street. Then she told him to be happy. Men were pigs, and now he could have the pleasure of living like one.

"It fits you perfectly."

Trying to keep some sort of sanity and stability, the boy spent most of his days with Hector and Victoria. He no longer gave the eggs to his momma, and since no one ate them, there were piling up beside the enclosure. The boy liked to mash them with his fingers or dig his nails through the shell and then wiggle a finger around inside of the gooey mass.

It was also around that same time he began hanging out with the neighbor's cat. He lured it close by handing it some of the ham his mother had put out for him in the burning heat, causing it to bulge and sweat. As the cat came to eat it, the boy grabbed the cat by its tail and brought it inside the shed with him. The cat became his friend, and he didn't even realize that the neighbors might have been missing it.

It wasn't until weeks later when the neighbor was looking for the cat, and his mother came inside the shed and found it with him. The boy was feeding it some of his food, while the cat kept him company. At first, he had thought that his mother would start to yell at him, but she didn't. Instead, she bent down, grabbed the cat in her arms, then left without even a word. It wasn't until the next day that his punishment came for stealing the cat.

The boy was still asleep when he heard the footsteps outside the shed, and then the door being forcefully pulled open. Barely had he opened his eyes on this Saturday morning before someone grabbed his arm and pulled him off the mattress and onto the floor, then dragged him outside. The boy had gotten pretty tall over the past year and was big for his age, but his momma could still give him a proper beating if she wanted to.

But that was not her intention on this crisp winter morning. She wanted to punish him, yes, and he knew she would as soon as he spotted the dead cat lying in the grass.

"Why did you take the cat?" his momma asked. "What were you going to do with it?"

When he didn't answer, she slapped him across the head, hard, and he screamed.

"It…I just wanted company. I feel so alone when I am out here when I come home from school," he yelled to make her stop hitting him. "I didn't mean to hurt anyone; I'm sorry."

His mother looked at him, then tilted her head. She took in a deep breath.

"What were you going to do with it, huh? Something filthy, am I right?"

"No! No! I wasn't…I mean…"

But it didn't matter what he said. His mother had made up her mind. She grabbed him by the arm and dragged him across the yard till they reached the enclosure, then she stopped. The boy stared at Victoria and Hector, then began to whimper.

"No, Momma. Please…no."

His momma answered with a smile, then grabbed the ax that was leaned up against the fence but hadn't been used since he and his dad built it.

"*Ple-e-a-s-e*…please…Momma!"

"Watch, boy. You hear me? Watch."

His momma then walked inside and grabbed Victoria first by the throat. The chicken squealed and cried out, trying to wiggle itself loose, but his momma held it tightly around its neck, then carried it outside, placed the chicken on the tiles, lifted the ax, and as the boy screamed, she chopped its head off. The boy stared at the head as it rolled across the tiles and the blood spurted out from what was left of it in his momma's hand.

His momma smiled. "There. Now, hand me the second one."

He shook his head. "No, Momma, no, please… don't…please."

"Go, boy. NOW!"

Shaking heavily, the boy walked inside, crying his heart out. He reached down and grabbed Hector in his hands and carried him out to his mother. The bird squirmed and squealed, sounding to the boy like it was crying for help, but his mother grabbed it mercilessly and chopped its head off.

The boy screamed as Hector's head landed next to Victoria's. He fell to his knees, crying.

That night, the boy was allowed to eat inside the house for the first—and last time—in many years. He sat at the table, and his mother looked at him, watching his every move, and made sure he swallowed every last bite of his chicken soup.

CHAPTER FIFTY-THREE

I was eight years old when I decided I wanted to kill my mother. I guess that's why I kill women, especially mothers. I am killing her over and over again. It really doesn't take a genius to figure out. See, my mother was as mean as they get. She deserved what she got. She deserved every bit of it. And she knew perfectly well it was me when I finally did kill her. She recognized her boy's hands and the eyes behind the mask. And she knew she had it coming. She knew her past had finally come back to haunt her.

Killing her was the best fix of my life. None of what I have done since has ever been able to give me as great a kick as that one did. Some of them have come close, I agree, but not close enough. I guess that's why I feel like I have to continue. The demand is growing inside of me to a point where I have to give into it again. I know I will have to.

The closest I ever came to feeling as big of a thrill as killing my mother was around ten years after I had started out. I had been taking a break for two years, letting things settle down a little, letting the police think I had moved on or maybe stopped, forcing them to focus on something else.

I was on my way home from work when I saw her. Actually, to be completely honest, I was stalking someone else that I had my heart set on. I had been following her for a few weeks, wondering if she was going to be my next one when I saw this brown-haired beauty walking up her driveway. I was still in my uniform, and I watched her as she walked inside her house. I drove slowly past her house and nodded at a neighbor who was grateful for my uniform. While wearing it, I could do as I pleased. No one ever thought it was strange that a guy like me drove around their neighborhood taking a closer look at the houses.

I watched her in my mirror as she went inside with her young boy and I knew it had to be her. She was too perfect to let go.

I was so infatuated with her that I got careless. This one looked so much like my mother; I didn't even stalk her for long before I had to give in to my desire. I didn't know her routine; I didn't even know if she had a boyfriend. I was just so obsessed with her; I knew I had to act soon. I didn't even go inside her house like I usually did when I knew my projects were at work or maybe sometimes just asleep. I did, however, send her flowers on the Friday before I struck.

Monday morning, I walked up to her house and simply walked right in through the front door. It always amazes me how people can keep their front doors locked all night, but not in the mornings after they go to pick up the paper. I was so blinded by my fascination with this woman, I didn't even care if the neighbors saw me. It didn't matter at that point. I had been doing this for ten years now, and no one was even close to finding me. As I said, I became careless. I stopped paying attention to details, and that's when it becomes dangerous.

The woman knew exactly who I was when I entered her house and locked the door behind me. I could tell by the look on her face that she did. I guess the mask gave me away. She told her son to stay in his room, probably hoping—like so many before her—that I would spare the son if I had my way with her. But the kid couldn't live. We both knew that deep down inside.

The woman was nervous, so I let her smoke a cigarette before I killed her and then moved on to the boy. I don't want to get into silly gory details, but it was my best kill—next after my mother's. Why it was so good, I can't explain. Maybe because it was so clean, so easy. Maybe because she was the one of my victims that resembled my mother the most. Maybe I was just really needy; I don't know. But I fantasized about that kill for many years afterward, especially since

I had to cool down afterward. As it turned out, a neighbor had seen me walk inside the house that morning, and soon a sketch was made of the possible Monday Morning Killer. It wasn't a very good sketch and looked nothing like me, but I realized that I had screwed up. I hadn't been careful enough, and it was time to cool down for a period. So, I did. I blended in. I became normal.

But it's tough. Imagine restraining from alcohol and sex and sugar all at once for years. Most people can't even cut out coffee from their daily diet. This demanded all my restraint. You know how us killers are. As soon as the last victim has fulfilled his or her purpose, then, sooner or later, we have to find a new victim to satisfy our need. As time passes, the pressure grows until we have to find some means of release. It's not a matter of free will. I am forced to take action, forced to kill again.

Soon.

CHAPTER FIFTY-FOUR

August 2018

I parked on the street outside the house and got out. I hadn't called ahead since I was afraid of Jim's reaction. He hadn't been very fond of the police earlier in the process, and I believed it would be easier to persuade him to talk to me if we were face to face. I didn't know if he was home but thought I'd take the chance and simply stop by. It was still early morning, and I had my mom taking care of the kids, making sure they got to school and taking care of Tyler for the day since he couldn't go to the daycare center. He had kept me awake all night with his crying, and I was exhausted, but I knew I had to push through if I was ever to solve this case, and I was determined to do so. I couldn't stand more kids losing their mothers, more families being destroyed by this monster.

The house was one of those new cookie-cutter ones in a nice, well-trimmed neighborhood where you couldn't tell any one from the other next door. They were all painted in that same light grey color, and only the amount of palm trees and bushes in front of them served as a way to separate them.

Jim lived at the end of a cul-de-sac, and I walked up thinking it was a great place to raise children. It seemed very safe.

I rang the doorbell, and a woman opened the door. She had pretty blue eyes that looked at me from a pale face. Her dark hair was pulled back in a ponytail.

"Yes?"

"I'm detective Ryder. I'm looking for Jim Reynolds?"

"He's out right now, I'm afraid."

"Do you know when he'll be back?"

"He worked the night shift, so he should be home in about half an hour," she said and looked at her watch.

"That's right. He works for KDL-security, right?"

She nodded.

Like Dennis Woods, the guy who lives across the street from Diane. Could that mean something? Do they know each other?

"Say, do you mind if I wait? It's half an hour drive back. Maybe you have a cup of coffee? I feel exhausted, my kid kept me awake all night, running a fever."

"Sure. I have a yoga class at nine, but Jim should be home way before then," she said and opened the door.

I walked inside. The house opened up to high vaulted ceilings. "I'm afraid I didn't even introduce myself," the woman said and turned to shake my hand. "My name is Laurie. I'm Jim's girlfriend, but I guess you kind of figured that out by now, or you'd be a lousy detective." She continued into the kitchen, and I followed her.

"I guess I would," I said with a chuckle.

The kitchen was brand-new with granite countertops all over and stainless-steel appliances. It was a little dark because of the closed blinds, which they probably kept closed to keep out the sun and the heat. Laurie turned on the lights and walked to a coffee maker.

"How do you like it? I can make a latte if you like."

"However you prefer to make it. I'm not difficult."

"Latte it is, then," she said and poured milk into a container of the machine. It was one of those fancy ones like they had at the cafés downtown. Shannon had bought one for our house too, but I had never really used it. Now that I heard hers spurt and spray out foam, I wondered if maybe I should start. It smelled heavenly.

Laurie placed a cup in front of me that looked like something I could get at Starbucks.

"Thanks," I said and tasted it. It was just as heavenly as it smelled. "I needed that."

I glanced at a picture over the fireplace showing Jim in his security guard uniform.

"Say…does he hang out with others from his company?" I asked.

She shrugged. "There are a few of them that he likes to see. We do couples dinners sometimes, but most of them have kids, and we don't, so it's sometimes a little much. I don't really have much in common with them. But I like them."

"Does he know a guy named Dennis Woods?"

"Sure," she said, happily. "Dennis and Camille? We see them at least once a month."

"So, you've been to his house out on Suwannee

Lane?" I asked, not exactly knowing where I was going with this.

"Oh, boy, yes. A million times. Well, not exactly, but you know what I mean," she said.

"Have you been out there recently?"

She nodded. "Yeah, they have this event once a year, this block party that he invited us to. We went there for that. It was fun."

I sipped my cup, wondering if it was just a coincidence. I had a feeling the Monday Morning Killer had been triggered by the fact that Diane had moved back into her house. Having studied for years how serial killers worked, I knew it could be the reason why it had all started over again. If I was right, then I also believed Diane was in grave danger merely by being in the house. I knew a killer like him was continually looking to relive his first fix, his first high, and even though he might have been able to keep himself bottled up for many years now, seeing Diane in that house would make him lose his cool. It was like waving a red flag in front of a bull. It woke him up. I was happy I had gotten her out. She was staying with my parents in one of their empty rooms at the motel, for free of course. 'Cause that's just how my parents were. Always generous, always ready to lend a helping hand to anyone in need.

I looked around the kitchen while drinking the coffee. On the fridge, I saw school pictures of Parker and his sister, Olivia. But they were old. The kids were both very young in the pictures; Parker looked to be around eight, maybe nine.

Laurie saw me staring at the pictures.

"It's so sad," she said. "What happened to them. Broke Jim's heart."

I nodded. "Do you get along with the kids? I know from personal experience how hard it can be when someone brings children into a relationship."

She sighed and sipped her own cup. "I hardly know them; I have to admit. I met Jim a year ago and, as much as he spoke about the children, I thought they were very close, but he hardly ever gets to see them. Amber won't let him…or wouldn't. I guess she figured since he was the one who left, then he made his choice. I think she was so angry with him for leaving that she decided to punish him by keeping the children from him, but it's not fair, you know? Jim loves those two, and now…well, he only has Parker left. Jim's been out there every day to be with him. We're getting the room upstairs ready for him so he can come and live here with us as soon as he is discharged."

I nodded and put the cup down on the counter. "And you're okay with Parker coming here to live?"

"Oh, absolutely. To be honest, I think it might make things easier for us. Jim misses them so much that it has often put a strain on our relationship. He can sometimes stay awake all night worrying about them, especially about the boy. He needs a man around, you know? Boys need a role model. And he had no one. Amber just kept him away from Jim."

"But surely Jim must have rights," I said and leaned forward.

Laurie gave me a look, and in that instant, I realized I had made a mistake.

CHAPTER FIFTY-FIVE

August 2018

"If he still has a fever tomorrow, then you should probably take him to the pediatrician."

My mom greeted me on the porch at the motel. Tyler was sleeping in her bedroom she told me when I came back from work later that same evening. I nodded in agreement, but at the same time thinking there was no way I had time to spend half a day in the doctor's office.

My mom gave me a look. She was setting the table for the entire family, even putting down a plate for Emily. She always did that, just in case the girl decided to come. My mom never gave up hope, that was one thing I could say about her.

"What?" I asked when seeing that look in her eyes.

"Don't you think it's time to throw in the towel?" she asked. "Stop trying to be a superhero?"

"What do you mean?"

"You can't do this alone, Jack. Those kids, especially Tyler. They need their mother around. You need your wife. There are six of them. You need an extra hand. Especially now that Tyler is sick. Not to mention Emily who needs you more than ever. It's okay not to be able to do all of that on your own."

"What do you want me to do about it?" I asked, annoyed that my mom wouldn't leave this alone. "Shannon is away on tour."

"You call her and tell her to come home. Tell her she's needed and that her career will have to wait a couple of years, at least till the kids are older and can take care of themselves. The fans and the fame will still be out there. It's not going anywhere. Besides, she can't have both. If she wants a family life, she has to choose the family. And that means sacrificing something else. Or at least putting it on hold."

I stared at my mother, whose look had changed to an expression of anger. She was obviously angry with Shannon and, as she said the words, I realized

I was too. I had been ever since she told me she was going away. I just had no idea how to say it to her because it felt selfish. But I was. I was furious that she had chosen her career over us, over her own family. I knew we could just have hired a nanny, but I felt like a failure to have strangers take care of my children. They were with other adults all day in school or daycare; I couldn't bear them having to be with one when they came home too.

But even though I felt this resentment toward Shannon for leaving, I also wanted to be a supportive husband at the same time. I wanted her to nurture her career and do what made her happy. But my mom was right. I couldn't do this alone. It wasn't fair to my mother either because it all ended up being her problem too. But I couldn't tell her that. I couldn't agree with her instead of my wife. I had to be loyal, so instead of telling her the truth, I just gave her an annoyed look.

"Well, maybe we do things a little differently, okay? We try the best we can, but times are different than when you had children, Mom. This is a new generation."

"The selfish generation," my mom said with a loud snort. "All about me-me-me. Never what is best for the children."

I sighed. "Things are different now; can we just leave it at that?"

My mom answered with another snort, then turned on her heel and walked back inside. Diane came out just as she did, then approached me.

"What was that all about?"

"Don't ask," I said, a little angrier than I had intended. Annoyed, I grabbed a chair and sat down. Diane exhaled. She walked back inside, then came out holding two beers between her hands. She handed me one, grabbed a chair, and sat down next to me.

"Cheers," she said, and we clanked bottles while staring at the ocean. There was a little swell coming in from the north, but I didn't even have the energy to think about surfing.

I was too tired and too pissed.

CHAPTER FIFTY-SIX

August 2018

Shannon was skipping as she walked through the airport, flanked by her security guards. She was so excited, probably the most excited she had been in a very long time.

She got into the limo waiting for her outside the building, holding the crate close to her body as she sat down.

She told the driver where she was going, and the limo took off. Shannon looked at her watch. It was evening but not yet dark out. This would be perfect timing.

Shannon grabbed her purse, then took out the pill bottle and popped another one to make sure her hand wouldn't mess up the night. She was planning on having a great time tonight.

She had the driver stop in the parking lot by the motel, then got out. He took her suitcases to the lobby and, as Shannon walked inside, she spotted them all sitting on the porch, eating.

Perfect timing.

This is going to be the best surprise ever.

Shannon could hardly contain her excitement as she grabbed the crate and walked outside.

"He-ello-o-o-o," she sang like she was still on stage.

The chatting subsided. All eyes were on her and jaws were dropped until the realization sank in. It happened with the children first.

"Mom?" Angela said.

"Mommy!" Tyler exclaimed, excited. He was kicking his small legs in the high chair, trying to get down. When he couldn't, he began to squeal, and his grandmother helped him get down so he could run to Shannon. A second later, she had put the crate down and grabbed the boy in her arms. She almost lost her balance on her high heels but regained it.

"Sh-Shannon?"

Jack stared at her, baffled. She chuckled. Of course, he was surprised.

"I had a day off, so I thought I'd come home and say hello," she squealed. "Flew in about an hour ago."

Jack looked at her like he didn't believe it. Angela threw herself into her mom's arms. "I missed you, Mommy. I'm so glad you're home."

It felt so good to hold her daughter in her arms again, and Shannon smelled her hair. Tyler had spotted the crate, and now he was wiggling to get loose from her grasp, then run to it and look inside.

"PUPPY!" the sound was so loud it cut through the air. "Puppy! Puppy! Puppy!"

That made all the children get up and rush to look for themselves. Austin and Abigail and Betsy Sue had no time to say hello to Shannon; the puppy completely over shone that.

"Can we take it out?" Abigail asked. "Pl-e-ease?"

"Yes, of course. It's ours now."

"We got a puppy?" Austin almost screamed.

Shannon nodded.

"Yes, silly. Why else would I bring it here, ha-ha."

Jack stood to his feet. "A puppy? What's going on here, Shannon?"

"What's going on? What's going on? I am here to see my family and I brought them a puppy. Isn't that a wonderful surprise?"

"We can't…we can't take care of a puppy… Why would you bring us a puppy?"

Shannon clapped her hands together like she hadn't heard him. "Oh, dinner. I'm starving. Did you save some for me?" She looked at the many faces staring back at her. Among them was a set of eyes that she didn't know.

"Uh. We have a visitor?" she said and approached her, almost tripping over a chair on her way. "So, who do we have here? I don't believe we've met."

The woman reached out her hand, and they shook.

"I'm…I'm Diane."

"Diane? Oh, DIANE," she squealed. "So, *you're* Diane…I see, well isn't this…nice, you're all sitting there…my kids…my family and…Diane."

Jack approached her. He got very close. It felt uncomfortable, and Shannon took a step back, almost falling.

"Aren't you happy to see me, not even an eensy teensy bit?

Shannon showed a little bit with her fingers, then giggled at her own joke. She was seriously working on making it something people said. She figured if she said it enough times, it would eventually catch on.

"What's wrong, Jack?" she said. "You look weird. What's wrong with your nostrils?"

"What's wrong with me?" Jack said. "What's wrong with *me*?"

He pulled off her sunglasses and looked closely at her eyes. Then he let out an angry scoff.

"You're high. You think a life in the force hasn't taught me what it looks like when someone's high? What the heck is going on with you, Shannon? You're getting high now?"

She rubbed her own arms anxiously. "I thought…I thought you'd be happy."

He took her purse. "What are you on?"

Jack searched inside her bag, then grabbed a bottle of pills. He looked up at her, and that awful look of disappointment was in his eyes. Shannon tried to blink, but it didn't go away. None of it would go away.

"These are opioids, Shannon," he said. "Are

you insane? With your history of alcohol abuse? How did you even get these?"

"A…a doctor," she said. "My doctor."

"What kind of a doctor would give you these?"

"My old doctor from Tennessee."

"Dr. Stanton gave you these? I can't believe him. He knows you're an alcoholic."

"But my hand was hurting, Jack…I couldn't play…they made the pain go away…"

Jack stared at her, then let out a deep sigh. "I can't even…I can't even look at you right now."

Jack reached out his arms with a loud groan, and without another word, he took off.

CHAPTER FIFTY-SEVEN

August 2018

I walked down to the beach and began to run. I had no clue where I was going, but I knew I just had to get away from there, away from all the craziness, away from all my anger. I was trying to run it out of my system, but about two miles down the beach, I realized it wasn't helping, and I stopped.

I had reached downtown and the restaurant Coconuts on the Beach, which was the only restaurant located directly on the beach in our little town. There was music playing from up there, so I went up on the porch and ordered myself a beer.

"Keep the tab open," I told the bartender.

I knew it wasn't the smartest thing to do, but if

Shannon could just give up on everything, then why couldn't I?

I sat by the railing facing the ocean and drank my Shock Top. While trying to digest all that was happening, I stared at the pills that were still in my hand with Shannon's name on the side of the bottle. I felt such deep anger rise inside of me. I couldn't believe her. How long had she been on these pills? Why on earth did she take them in the first place? She knew her own history. She knew she would never be able to control it and, worst of all, so did the people around her. Bruce, Dr. Stanton, Sarah? Even Sarah should have known better. Why hadn't she stopped her? Were they all so hung up on making money they didn't care about her health? It was like she was some puppet.

I was sipping my beer while looking out over the ocean when my phone rang. It was my mom.

"You done running from your problems yet?" she asked.

I took in a deep breath. "In a few minutes."

"Good, 'cause you're needed here. Shannon has passed out on the couch in the common room, and the kids need to get to bed. It's way past their bedtime. Diane has taken them back to your place. Your dad and I are exhausted, to be honest."

Hearing my mother's voice made me lose it. Suddenly, tears were spilling down my cheeks, and I couldn't stop them.

"I'm…I don't know what to do, Mom."

She exhaled. "I know, son. But you won't find your answer at the bottom of a beer, let me tell you that. Come home. Let Shannon sleep it off and then figure out what to do. But come home. The kids need their dad. They've just seen their mom and stepmom completely lose it, and they're scared, Jack. They need your stability, your strength. I know it's tough to have to pick up the broken pieces over and over again, but that's what parents do. Heck, I still do it for you."

"I know, Mom. I know."

"Good, now be a man and come take care of your family. There's no time to sit and feel sorry for yourself. You can do that when the kids leave for college, and the house is empty."

My mom hung up, and I wiped my tears away. I lifted my glass with the intention of finishing the beer but then decided that wasn't doing anyone any good and put it back down.

PART FOUR

CHAPTER FIFTY-EIGHT

August 2018

I felt like I was drowning. Literally. Piles of files, new and old ones were occupying my desk among old coffee cups and leftover sandwiches. Meanwhile, I was trying to focus on reading everything, going through every detail of the old cases, looking for anything that might tell me more about this Monday Morning Killer and his ways, maybe even find a little mistake or a detail I hadn't focused on before. And, so far, I had found one. In his last kill, before he cooled down for thirty-four years—as far as we know—he had been seen walking into the victim's house by a neighbor. The neighbor had assumed he was visiting since he walked straight in without even knocking and didn't think any more of it, not until he saw all the police cars in the street later in the day when returning from work. He had then told the police that the man he saw walk inside the house was wearing a uniform. What kind of uniform, he couldn't tell. He only had sight in one of his eyes since the right one was lazy and he only had like eighty percent vision in the good one, but the uniform had an emblem on the shoulder, he had said.

"Like the one a security guard wears," I mumbled to myself and thought about Jim Reynolds. He was old enough to fit the description. Plus, he had a pretty good motive for wanting Amber Reynolds dead. I just wasn't so sure that this killer needed a motive. His kills weren't random; they were carefully planned out, but it didn't seem like he was getting revenge with each and every victim, more like with someone else that he couldn't kill or already had killed.

I sighed and leaned back in my chair. I rubbed my forehead. I couldn't really concentrate. My thoughts kept returning to Shannon and her behavior the night before.

My mom had put her in one of her rooms for the night, and I had gotten up this morning and sent the kids off to school and day-care without even checking in on her.

Maybe I should have; I don't know. I wasn't really ready to face her yet. So, instead, I buried myself in my work, even though I was only doing so halfheartedly. I knew my mom would make sure Shannon—and the puppy—were well taken care of and that I'd have to face her later in the day.

I just didn't know what to say.

I felt so angry it was like I was about to explode, and then I was heartbroken at the same time. I wanted to yell at her, scold her for being so stupid, and then hug her and hold her tight, and tell her it was going to be all right. All at the same time. I loved the woman, dang it. I just wasn't sure how much more of this I could bear. How much the kids could take. They had seen her, how she acted yesterday. I couldn't hide it from them. They knew something was wrong, especially Angela, who had grown up while watching her mother drink herself half to death. The girl had to be devastated.

"I never should have let her go," I mumbled to myself. "I knew it was a bad idea as soon as she told me about the tour. I felt it, deep inside."

"What's that?"

I lifted my head and met Joe Hall's eyes above the stacks of files.

"Oh, hey, man. I didn't see you there. What's up?"

"I have something you need to see. At the Reynolds' house."

I rose to my feet. "You found something?"

"Well, it was actually the crime scene techs, but I was there, and so they told me to go get you."

I grabbed my phone along with my gun and badge and left the desk, feeling quite relieved to get away for a little while. I needed it. I felt stuck.

CHAPTER FIFTY-NINE

August 2018

"I've messed up everything. How is that even possible in so short of an amount of time?"

Diane looked at herself in the rearview mirror. She hadn't slept at all last night. She had kept wondering about Jack and Shannon and how she felt like she had come between them. It was the last thing she ever wanted to do. She cared for Jack, yes, she had to admit she did. And maybe even a little more than as a friend. And that wasn't healthy.

"Why did I even come here?" she said, then backed out of the parking lot behind the motel. Jack had been so nice as to pick up her car the afternoon before and, luckily, it had been able to start once he tried and it did so again this morning, much to Diane's relief.

She had gathered all her things—which wasn't much—that she had brought to the motel and put it in the trunk. She hadn't even said goodbye to Sherri and Albert, and she wasn't going to. They would only try and convince her to stay and ask her where she would go, and she couldn't deal with that right now. All she knew was that she had to get away, as far away from Cocoa Beach as possible.

"It was a mistake to come here. It was a huge mistake," she told herself as she rushed down A1A. "Why are you so stupid, Diane? Why?"

She shook her head and slammed her hand against the steering wheel. She couldn't blame Shannon for being upset. She really couldn't. Had she felt satisfied and at home with Jack's family? Yes, that's exactly how she had felt sitting there on the porch at the motel, enjoying Sherri's wonderful cooking and seeing all those smiling faces. She had felt at home, and she had so desperately wished it was. For just a second, she had allowed herself to dream that she was the one who had married Jack and was living on the beach with him, that she was the mother of his many children and that he loved her still. For just one unforgiving second, she had dreamt it. Just like she used to dream that she was a real part of his family when growing up, when her dad came home drunk and started throwing things, and she sought shelter at Jack's house. Back then, she had prayed to God that he would make her a part of their family. This was the only place she had ever felt at home. With them.

But it was all a lie, and now she was facing the consequences. There was no way she could ever have what they had. It just wasn't in her cards.

Misty made a sound from the back seat, and Diane looked at her in the rearview mirror.

"I know," she said and drove through downtown, toward the north side of town. "I wanted to stay too. But we can't destroy Jack's life. He has a good thing going there, and we can't get in the way of that. He loves his wife and he should. I just hope she knows how to appreciate him, appreciate the life she has with him."

Diane drove off A1A and into Suwannee Lane, then up toward her house. She would just get her things for now, the little she had brought with her when she came. Later, she would contact Mary Hass, the real estate agent, and ask her to sell the house for her again. Maybe there was still one sucker left out there who didn't know the story of the murder house.

CHAPTER SIXTY

August 2018

I parked the car in the driveway, and we got out. A crime scene tech approached us.

"It's in the back," he said.

We walked around the house, following him closely.

"We were almost done in the house when we saw it. I guess we didn't think of going inside until now, maybe because we assumed it was just for surfboards. But I'm glad we did," he said and turned to look at me. "I don't know if it is important, but I thought you should see it."

I nodded and followed him to a slim surf shed in the backyard. He opened the door and held it for me.

"It's in here."

I stepped inside. There wasn't much to see, but what I saw was enough.

"It looks like someone has been sleeping in here," the tech said and pointed at the mattress on the ground. It was all very dirty, and bugs were crawling on the floors and walls.

There wasn't much else in there but the mattress on the floor and some clothing on a chair in the corner.

"It's like a sauna in here," Joe Hall said and untucked the shirt of his uniform. "There's no AC?"

The tech shook his head.

"How on earth has anyone been sleeping in here without AC?" Joe asked.

I looked around at the dirty shed and felt the sweat springing to my forehead. I grabbed a shirt from the chair and looked at it.

"The question we need to ask is *why*," I said. I turned to look at Joe Hall. "Why would anyone sleep out here?"

I knelt next to the bed and felt it. There wasn't even a sheet on it. It was stained and dirty.

"Could it have been a homeless person?" Joe asked.

I reached under the pillow and pulled out an old notebook, then smiled while waving it in the air.

"That's what we're about to find out."

CHAPTER SIXTY-ONE

August 2018

Diane parked the car in front of her house and got out. She took Misty with her, so the cat wouldn't die of heat stroke in the car while she gathered her things. She didn't know how long it would take, but she hoped it wouldn't be too long.

She just needed to get out of here. And fast.

Mr. Fogerty came out on his porch when she walked up. He was wearing his dogcatcher uniform, holding a cup of coffee in his hand. His eyes watched her as they always did, and she smiled in greeting, yet couldn't help feeling a chill run down her spine as his eyes continued to stare. The man didn't smile back, and Diane rushed to her front door. She grabbed the handle and unlocked the door, thinking she couldn't wait to get away from this place and its creepy neighbors.

Inside the house, she felt the unease come over her as she always did, and she hurried up the stairs, putting Misty down so he could roam while she packed up her clothes. She only had about two suitcases to pack. It shouldn't take long.

After that, she'd get the few plates she had brought, the ones she had inherited from her aunt. She wouldn't want to leave them here. Where she was going, she would surely have a use for those.

Wherever she was going.

You need a plan. You can't just take off.

Diane didn't have a plan. She had no idea if she would drive north or south, east or west. Where could she possibly hide? It'd have to be in a place Frank would never think of looking for her. She didn't even know if her car could get her anywhere. It was old and not very reliable.

Take it one day at a time. That's all you can do right now.

Diane nodded as she reached the end of the stairs. There really wasn't more to it than that, taking it day-by-day, hour-by-hour. Something would turn up; something always did along the way.

She just had to focus on what she was doing right now and nothing else.

Diane walked down the hallway and reached the door to her bedroom, then opened it. As she saw what—or rather who—waited for her on the other side, sitting on top of her bed, she almost instantly stopped breathing.

CHAPTER SIXTY-TWO

August 2018

I was pulling my hair while reading the notebook. I had gone back to my office and moved a couple of files to make room for it on my desk, then grabbed a cup of coffee and started reading. But what I found in there made me so sick to my stomach I couldn't even finish the coffee.

"Anything useful?" Joe asked as he approached me.

I looked up.

"You look a little pale," Joe said. "You okay?"

I swallowed. "I…I don't think so."

"You don't think you're all right or you don't think you found anything useful?" he asked.

"Maybe both," I said. "I don't really know what to say to this."

Joe sipped his cup, still standing and looking down at me. "What is it? What's written in it?"

"I…I'm not too sure…yet," I said and looked out the window at the traffic on A1A rushing by. My thoughts were running wild as I thought about what I had read, what I was holding between my hands. There was something I seemed to be missing about this case, something about this book and the mattress in the shed and the way Mrs. Reynolds was decapitated when none of the other victims were.

"So, you don't think we can use it to crack the case, then?" Joe asked.

I turned and looked at him again. "No, I think that's exactly what we can use it for."

Joe gave me a puzzled look. "You're not making much sense here, Jack. You sure you don't need to go home and rest? You don't look too well, to be perfectly honest."

I shook my head as another piece of the puzzle seemed to fall into place. "I think…"

I stopped then and looked up at Joe. I stood to my feet, still holding the notebook in my hand.

"Come with me."

"Come with me, *please*," Joe corrected me with a

grin, but I ignored him. As I rushed out of the building housing the station, my heart was racing so loudly in my ears that it drowned out everything else. If I was right in my theory, then there was no time to waste.

CHAPTER SIXTY-THREE

August 2018

"Frank?"

Diane's heart sank as she looked at her ex-husband sitting on her bed. He was looking at her, smiling from ear to ear.

"W-what are you doing here?"

"What am I doing here?" he asked. "What am *I* doing here? I think I'm the one who should ask you that question. What on earth are *you* doing in this God-forsaken place? In this…house? I don't even know if I should call it that. What is this place?"

Diane backed up and held onto the door behind her.

"How did you find me?"

Frank saw her slowly backing up and stood to his feet. "Does it matter?"

"Yes, it matters. W-why have you come? Why are you here?" Diane asked, wondering if she could run for the knives in the kitchen fast enough. She risked him catching her on her way down the stairs.

"I'm here to take you home," he said.

"This is my home now," she said.

Frank laughed. "This place? You can't seriously tell me you're living here?"

She swallowed. "Well, I am."

He shook his head. "That's actually how I found you. Your real estate agent was so kind as to post a picture on Facebook when she sold you the house. One of my old army buddies saw it and sent it to me asking if we had split up. Do you have any idea how humiliating that was, huh?"

Frank was getting aggressive now, and Diane took another step back, still wondering about the knives in the block downstairs. She had moved them, so they were now by the fridge, next to the microwave. She could reach them if she hurried. Frank wouldn't touch her if she threatened to stab him, would he? She realized she had no idea what he was capable of or how he would react to that. But at least she'd be able to protect herself.

He won't hurt me, will he? What about the baby?

"I don't care, Frank. I'm divorcing you. It's over."

She might as well have punched him in the face. The look in his eyes changed drastically, and he reached out to grab her, but she was faster than him, and as he jumped forward, she turned around and ran for the stairs. Running as fast as she could, she took the stairs two steps at a time, but she felt a push on her back, and she flew down the stairs and landed face-first on the new tiles.

Diane rose to her knees. She felt her stomach while crying.

Please, be okay; please, let the baby be okay.

Diane managed to grab onto the counter and pull herself up. She looked down at her pants. She didn't feel anything warm or see any blood. Her shoulder had taken the brunt of the fall and was hurting badly, but better that than her stomach.

Anything but the baby.

Frank laughed from the top of the stairs, then started to walk down. Diane coughed in pain and got up. From where she was standing, she could see the block of knives at the other end of the kitchen.

"Diane, Diane, Diane," Frank said while walking toward her. "You'll never get rid of me.

Never. You can run all you want to, but I will always find you."

Diane panted with pain and stared at the knives. While Frank made his little speech, she rushed to them, sprang for them, grabbed a handle and pulled one out. Panting and wheezing, she turned toward him, pointing the knife at him.

"Don't you dare take one step closer. I will kill you, Frank. I will."

Frank stared at the knife as he took the last step into the kitchen. He looked at it, then up at Diane again, then began to laugh.

"You think I'm scared of dying? Death doesn't frighten me. Losing you does. Losing you and the baby is the only thing that I'm afraid of."

As he spoke, Frank pulled out a gun from his pants pocket. His hand holding the gun was shaking violently as he pointed it at Diane. He smiled between tears that were now rolling down his cheeks.

"It'll be beautiful," he said. "We'll go together. All three of us reunited in death. If we can't be together in this life, then we will be in the next."

CHAPTER SIXTY-FOUR

August 2018

Jim Reynolds turned and looked at me as we entered. His eyes were puzzled.

"Detective?"

"Mr. Reynolds," I said, and Joe closed the door behind us.

"What can I do for you? Why are you here?" His voice was shaking lightly as he looked at me, then at Joe, then back at me.

"What's going on?" Parker said. He was sitting up in the hospital bed but was dressed in ordinary clothes. Jim Reynolds was packing his backpack with all the cards and boxes of chocolate he had received while in the hospital.

"I don't know," Jim said. "Maybe Detective Ryder and his colleague have come to wish you good luck now that you're being discharged."

"Not exactly, I'm afraid," I said.

"Well, maybe they're here to say they found out who killed your mother and your sister then," Jim said. "I-is that why you're here, Detective, huh?"

I nodded.

"Well, that is amazing news, then," Jim exclaimed. "Why the long face, Detective?"

"Because I'm looking at the killer," I said.

Jim Reynolds gasped and held his chest. "What on earth are you talking about, Detective? I don't understand. I've told you a million times, I…"

And that was when he realized I wasn't looking at him but at Parker.

Jim Reynolds scoffed. He looked at the boy, then at me. He was shaking his head in disbelief.

"This time, you've gone too far, Detective. This is insane, Parker; you shouldn't listen to…"

The boy looked down first, then lifted his gaze up at Jim. Jim took a step backward.

"It's…is this true?"

"I'm afraid so," I said.

Jim Reynolds stumbled backward and sat in a chair behind him, eyes wide open.

"But…how? Why? I thought…I thought you were looking for someone who killed someone… forty years ago? It makes no sense?"

"We were, and we are," I said. "But whoever killed those people didn't kill Parker's mother and sister. Parker did." I paused, then addressed the boy. "They treated you like hell, didn't they? It didn't occur to me until I saw the shed. The clothes there were your size. You hated her, didn't you? You hated your mother for pushing your father away. For treating you like dirt and making you sleep in the shed."

"She hated me," the boy said. He wasn't looking at me when he spoke. His glare landed on the wall right next to me, like he was seeing it all once again in some invisible movie playing on the white wall that only he could see.

"She hated all men. You know how she was," he said addressed to Jim. "She made me sleep in the shed. She beat me, and she…she killed Victoria and Hector. She chopped their heads off and made me watch. Then she made soup with the heads and made me eat it."

"That was why you chopped her head off as well. That was the part I couldn't get to fit with the Monday Morning Killer," I said. "He had never done anything like that before. He had used belts and plastic bags, but always strangled people. He had never mutilated any bodies."

Parker nodded. "I know."

"But…but he was hurt," Jim said. "He was hit by several cars."

"You got scared, didn't you?" I asked. "Killing them wasn't exactly how you imagined it, and then you freaked out, didn't you?"

Parker began to sob. "I got so scared. My sister, she begged for her life, she cried and screamed, and it wasn't so bad as long as she did that; it was when she stopped that I got scared."

"Because now there was no way back," I said. "So, when you realized she was dead, you ran, you ran as fast as you could into ongoing traffic, not even caring if you lived or died."

"I think I wanted to die," he said. "At that point, I just wanted to end it all. I wanted to be a killer; I wanted to be like the Monday Morning Killer, but I realized I could never be him."

Jim stared at Parker, breathing heavily, still shaking his head. "Why on Earth did you want to be like him?"

I exhaled and showed him the notebook.

"Because of this," I said. "At first, when I read it, I didn't understand. I mean, listen to this," I said and opened the book to a page and read out loud:

"I was eight years old when I decided I wanted to kill my mother. I guess that's why I kill women, especially mothers."

I closed the book again. "I kept thinking what the heck is this? That's what I asked myself, and then I realized, it's a book. A manuscript. Written by the Monday Morning Killer, telling about every kill he ever made and even why he did them and how he planned them."

"How did you get ahold of such a book?" Jim asked, startled.

"That's what I kept asking myself too. But I think I know where it came from. You found it, didn't you? In your mother's belongings."

Parker looked down, then nodded. "She kept it. It was in the box of things that she had in the garage."

"Containing all your father's stuff, am I right?"

Parker nodded. "I wanted to be just like him."

"His real name is Steve Carver," I said and pointed at the cover of the notebook where he had written his name. "For years and years, people believed he was the victim when his family was murdered up on Suwannee Lane, but in fact, he killed them all, didn't he? Then he told the police a story about the killer still being in the house and how he escaped him, and then told the same thing to the reporters. It made him famous. But then he realized killing his family, killing his mother wasn't enough. He had thought it would be, but the urges were still there. He knew he couldn't keep killing unless he changed his name. He had to become anonymous again, blend in. It was the only way he could keep killing without being noticed. So, he left town. He went away for a few years and came back with a new name, a new look, and a brand-new identity. Meanwhile, the town had forgotten all about him and moved on, and no one thought of looking for him since they believed he was gone. But he's been living among us ever since, looking for a fix that he only believes he can get here, where he had his first kill. He's been trying, again and again, to reach the same high that he got from killing his own mother. It's all in this book. Every little detail." I held up the notebook.

"She told me I was like him," Parker said, crying. "Said she could see it in my eyes. Called me evil and wouldn't let me even go near my sister or her. She was certain I had the evil inside of me." He looked up at Jim. "Just like my dad. So, I proved to her that she was right."

"So, she knew?" I asked.

He nodded.

Jim Reynolds stared at me, then at the boy, then back at me. He tried to speak, but no words seemed to leave his lips. I stepped toward him.

"It was while talking to Laurie, your girlfriend, that I realized I had been mistaken," I said. "I had just assumed you were the father, but you were just the husband. You weren't the father. You didn't come into their lives until they were already born. After Steve Carver left."

Jim nodded. "I was a father as much as anyone gets to be. I was there for them while growing up. They called me dad. But still she…it broke my heart when she kept them from me. I had to leave her because I couldn't be a witness to the way she treated Parker and I couldn't stand the way she treated me. I loved those children, but she wouldn't let me."

"And you had no rights."

I nodded at Joe, and he went to get Parker to take him back with us to the station. Jim Reynolds was sobbing as Joe escorted Parker, who came along willingly. I put my hand on Jim's shoulder.

"I'm so sorry," I said.

"I…I just don't…" He looked up. "But…but if Parker did…then who…who is the Monday Morning Killer, then?"

I exhaled. "That's what I have yet to figure out."

CHAPTER SIXTY-FIVE

August 2018

"Please…please, don't hurt me…" Diane said. "Don't hurt us."

"How…how could you do this to me?" Frank asked, pointing the gun at her. Tears were spilling down his cheeks. "We were so good together. We were the ones who were going to last, remember? Everyone said so."

"Please," she pleaded. "Please, just let me go. It doesn't have to end here. Not like this."

"But you're the one who did this. Don't you see? You killed us; you killed our baby. If you can't see that, then I really don't know what to do for you anymore. You're out of reach. I can't help you anymore."

"W-what are you talking about, Frank?" Diane whimpered. There was such madness in Frank's eyes that it terrified her.

"I have helped you, haven't I? I made you a better person. I made you better, Diane. You were a mess when we met, and I helped you. I took care of you, and this…this is how you thank me?"

Diane shook her head. "You're insane."

He stepped forward, and Diane gasped in shock.

"I'm not the one who's insane," he said. "You are. Don't you see what you do to me? What you make me do?"

She shook her head, crying. "Please, Frank. Please."

"I'm sorry, Diane. But this is our only chance. There's no way around it. It must be done, don't you see?"

Realizing there was nothing she could say or do to make him change his mind, Diane fell to her knees and dropped the knife. She closed her eyes and covered her ears, waiting for her destiny, for death to come and take her away.

As she heard the gunshot, she fell forward. Maybe it was instinctively; maybe she really thought she had been shot. But as the seconds passed and she felt no pain, she opened her eyes. As she did, she spotted Frank. He was on the floor, lying on her new tiles, his blood spilling from a wound in his chest.

Diane gasped and got to her knees, then looked behind her. In the doorway stood Dennis, still holding the gun between his hands. He was sweating heavily and stood like he was frozen, staring at the man he had just shot.

"D-Dennis?" she said.

Finally, he came to himself and looked at her, lowering the gun. "Diane. Are you all right? I…I saw you from the house, I saw the guy holding the gun and I just…" He looked at the gun in his hand. "I have it for emergencies, you know. When Camille is home alone and I am on a night shift."

Diane sprang toward him, then threw herself around his neck. "Thank you. Thank you. Thank you. You saved my life."

He looked baffled and a little proud. "Ah, well…it was nothing."

"To me, it sure was something," she said.

Dennis walked to the dead body and looked down at him. Diane felt her heart jump as she saw the body of her ex-husband in a pool of his own blood.

"I'll be…" Dennis said.

"You came just in time," she said.

"Was he the Monday Morning Killer?" he asked.

Diane looked at him, then shook her head. "He was my ex-husband. He came to get me back or maybe just to kill me; I don't know."

"I'll be…"

"I'll call for help."

Hands shaking, heart pounding, Diane grabbed her phone and once more dialed a number she had sworn she would never dial again.

CHAPTER SIXTY-SIX

August 2018

"Calm down, Diane. Tell it to me one more time; this time slower so I can follow you, please."

I was driving back to the station when she called. In the back seat, we had Parker. His stepdad was following in his own car. Parker was sobbing behind us as I drove into the parking lot, still talking to Diane who had called me sounding all frantic.

"Frank is dead. I'm looking at him here on my floor. He tried to kill me, Jack. It was him all along. He's known where I was all this time, ever since I bought this house. So, he was waiting for me when I got back. I was so scared, Jack."

"Wait…you went back to the house?" I asked

while Joe got out and escorted Parker to the station. I stayed in the car for a few more minutes trying to figure out what exactly was going on.

"I thought we agreed that you would stay away from that place till it was safe to go back?"

"We did, and I did, but then after all that happened last night, I decided to…well, I decided I had to get out of here, leave you two alone and not get between you anymore, so I went back home to get some stuff, you know clothes and so on, and then he was there. He was sitting on my bed, waiting for me, waiting to kill me."

"So, you're telling me all those things that happened, all those strange things, that was your ex?"

"Yes. It must have been him. He's known where I live ever since I moved in. It was him. I'm telling you."

"And now he's dead you say? How?" I asked feeling suddenly very awake. "Did you kill him?"

"No, it was Dennis. My neighbor from across the street. He saw Frank with the gun, then came to my rescue. He's sitting on my porch right now, and I don't know what to do. I'm freaking out. I don't think he's feeling very well, to be honest."

"Well, no wonder if he just killed a guy," I said.

This day just kept getting stranger and stranger. "Listen, Diane. I'll send someone, okay? Just don't touch anything. That's very important, okay?"

"Okay."

"Good. I'll send a patrol car. Now, are you okay?"

She paused like she was thinking, then said: "I don't know. I think I might have dislocated my shoulder when he pushed me down the stairs, but other than that, I think so."

"I was talking about you, Diane, not your body. Are you okay?"

She paused again.

"I'm not sure. Come to think of it, I do feel a little dizzy…like I need to throw up."

"That's the shock wearing off. The adrenaline has kept you going so far, but now that it's sinking in what really happened, you'll feel the consequences. Go sit down, and I'll send a patrol."

"You're not coming?" she asked.

I closed my eyes. "I…I'm kind of in the middle of something," I said. "We just brought a guy in for killing the Reynolds family. Things are kind of hectic right now."

"O-okay."

We hung up, and I walked inside where I found

Mike. "Could you send a patrol to Suwannee Lane?" I asked. "An intruder has been shot."

Mike looked up at me, surprised. "Let me guess. At your old girlfriend's place?"

I nodded. "I'm afraid so. Ex-husband. He tried to kill her."

"I'll be…and you're not going?"

I bit my lip. "Not right now. I'll wait till the techs are done."

"You sure about that?"

Mike looked into my eyes, and I could tell he was searching for answers. I couldn't really tell him the details and why I couldn't face Diane right now, but he seemed to understand. I was overwhelmed with guilt for letting her down in her time of need, but I simply couldn't. I was terrified of the feelings she had revived inside of me, especially now that Shannon was…I shook my head. No, I had to focus on my family right now.

"Okay, then. I don't have any patrols available right now. There was a big crash on 520, but I'll go myself."

I nodded. "I owe you one. Thanks, Mike."

"No problem."

CHAPTER SIXTY-SEVEN

August 2018

"There's a patrol coming," Diane said and walked back to Dennis, who was sitting in a chair on the porch, staring at his shoes.

The front door was still wide open and, as she glanced inside, she could see Frank's shoes. She took in a deep breath to calm herself down. She had never seen a dead person before, and the thought of him lying in there gave her goosebumps. She turned to look at Dennis instead, wondering why Jack wouldn't come and help her. She had really screwed up with him, hadn't she? As soon as all this was over, she was getting out of here.

"Are you okay?" she asked Dennis.

He rubbed the sides of his head, then nodded.

Diane exhaled. "My hands are still shaking," she said. "And my legs are kind of too."

Dennis made a strange sound and, at first, Diane believed he was crying. He sat with his head bent down toward his legs and his hands rubbing his temples, making what sounded like a sobbing sound, but soon changed into something else.

Is he laughing?

"Dennis?"

Dennis lifted his head and looked at her, grinning from ear to ear when he burst into full-blown laughter.

Why is he laughing? What's so funny and why is he looking at me weirdly like that?

"D-Dennis? You're kind of scaring me here. What's so funny?"

He shook his head. "Nothing. And everything, I guess."

Has he gone mad?

He grabbed the gun in his hand and looked at it.

"Maybe you should put that back down," she said. "It's evidence now."

He looked up at her, and their eyes met. There was a madness in them she hadn't seen in him before.

"I'm gonna be charged with murder, aren't I?" he said. "I'm gonna have to do time."

"No, no. It was self-defense. Plus, you're a security guard. You saved my life, remember?"

He got up to his feet and reached out for her. She didn't move fast enough, and Dennis grabbed her arm, tight.

"You owe me big time now; you do realize that, right?"

He was pressing himself uncomfortably toward her, but she couldn't get away. She could feel the gun between them. She could feel his breath on her face as he spoke.

"You know I could have had you. I should just have kissed you that other night when I cut your power line. I wanted you to come running to me. I wanted you to come knocking on my door for help. That was why I did it, but instead, you came running into the yard and took me off guard."

Diane stared at him, her heart pounding in her chest. "Y-you cut the power line?"

Dennis grinned goofily. "Heh. I thought you'd figured that one out when you met me." He used a hand to caress her cheek while pushing the gun toward her stomach. "I should have just kissed you right there. Lord knows I wanted to. But I was a chicken. I kept thinking this isn't the way it was supposed to happen. It has to be done right. I wanted it to be perfect."

Diane felt sweat spring on her upper lip. "W-what are you telling me, Dennis?"

"That I have wanted you since the day I first laid eyes on you. I knew I had to have you. A woman like you shouldn't be all alone in that awful old house. But then you kept hanging out with that detective, and he ended up sitting with you in the kitchen, comforting you on that night. It should have been me."

"You've been watching me? D-did you open all my cabinets and lock in my cat as well?" Diane asked. "And lie on my bed?"

"You liked that one, did you? The one with the cabinets? I thought that was very clever myself. The moving of your car was too. I wanted you to be scared, Diane, because I wanted you to come running to me for help. But you never did. I told you. Anything. I'll be happy to help, but you didn't want my help, did you? You kept running to that Jack Ryder fellow. Boy, that made me so MAD."

Diane whimpered as Dennis pressed himself against her. She closed her eyes and tried to turn her head away, but he grabbed her chin and forced her to turn her head toward him, then planted his lips on top of hers. He pushed his tongue into her mouth, and Diane felt like throwing up. He held her so tightly that she couldn't move, stuffing his tongue down her throat, when she heard a loud thud from behind him, and Dennis suddenly went numb. His tongue slid out of her mouth, and his hand let go of her chin as his eyes rolled back into his head and he fell onto the wooden porch with a loud plump sound.

Diane gasped and blinked. In front of her stood Mr. Fogerty, still wearing his dogcatcher uniform. His cheeks were blushing in agitation, his hair standing up sporadically.

Between his hands, he held a baseball bat. He looked at Dennis on the porch, then up at Diane while correcting his hair.

"Should've done that a mighty long time ago," he said and spat on the wood next to the unconscious Dennis. "You all right there, hon?"

Diane nodded with a whimper. "I...I think so."

"Good."

With a nod, he turned around and walked down the three steps to the grass, the bat swung over his shoulder, and returned to his house, where Diane heard the door slam shut.

She looked after him for quite some time, then down at Dennis, who soon started to moan. Diane gasped. Mr. Fogerty hadn't hit him half as hard as they had both thought and he was already waking up.

Diane turned to look toward Mr. Fogerty's house, wondering if he would be able to help her once again if she screamed, then decided she wasn't going to stick around to get the answer.

Diane bent down and grabbed the gun between two fingers, then ran inside, found her purse, put the gun inside the purse, then grabbed her cat under the other arm, and rushed to her car.

She watched as Dennis squirmed and moved on the porch, then sat up. Her heart pounded in her chest as she frantically put the key in the ignition and turned it.

The car coughed a few times, then stopped.

"Oh, no. Sweet, sweet car, please don't fail me now. Please don't."

But the car was dead. It wasn't even coughing anymore as she tried to start it and soon Dennis was on his feet, stumbling around until he gathered himself and spotted her inside the car. With an angry movement, he lunged toward her.

CHAPTER SIXTY-EIGHT

August 2018

I couldn't stop thinking about Diane and praying that she was okay. Facing her ex-husband in that manner had to be terrifying. I felt so guilty for not being there for her, but I simply couldn't. I had to stay away from her if I was going to save my marriage, and I wanted that more than anything in the world. I had played a weighty part of Shannon's demise. My taking in Diane and letting her have dinners at our house with my family must have been terrible for Shannon, especially since she was away. I knew Shannon had taken the pills herself; she was the one who had decided to put them in her body but knowing I was at home with my high school sweetheart played a huge part of her decision to do so. I knew it did. I had to take my part of the responsibility. I had triggered it and, from now on, I had to stay far away from Diane in order for it not to happen again. I had to be professional and, as it was, it would never have been me who was the first responder to a scene like that. It would always be a patrol. Then they would call me in later. That was the usual procedure, and I was sticking to it. It was tough, and it felt like I was hiding behind it, but this was what I had to do right now.

"I heard you caught the Reynolds' killer," a voice said coming from behind me. "Congratulations."

I looked up and saw Weasel.

"Joe filled me in," she said.

"I was going to tell you about it," I said, "but your secretary said you were in a meeting."

"So, it was the son, huh?" she asked. "Who'd have thought that?"

I nodded. "But that also means that the Monday Morning Killer is still out there," I said. "Somewhere."

Weasel smiled. "Don't look at what you haven't done yet. Celebrate your victories, Ryder. And this is one. No one could have cracked this case the way you did. I'm proud of you."

Those were big words coming from Weasel. I knew that much.

"And the mom knew, huh? She knew who he was? Why didn't she come to us?"

I shrugged. "Probably scared out of her wits. Finding out that you've married a serial killer and had his children can't be easy. She was probably terrified that he would come back and kill them all. Parker told us she was terrified of him, that she was afraid he was going to turn into the monster his dad was. That's why she couldn't stand him or having him around. That's why she told him to sleep in the shed."

"And in treating him that way, she actually did turn him into exactly that," Weasel said.

I nodded. "That's the irony of it all, I guess."

I glared out the window for a short second, then back at the piles on my desk. "I just can't help feeling that he's right…here. I can almost reach out and grab him, you know?"

"And I have a feeling you will," she said.

"All that time, I thought that what triggered him to resurface was the fact that someone, that Diane had moved into that old house. I thought that seeing someone living there again had made him lose it and start killing again. But that wasn't it. It was the fact that his son killed like him, that his son copied his first kill by killing his own mother. If you read the notebook, that was exactly what Steve Carver had fantasized about, that was why he killed. Because he hated his mother so deeply. And so, when his son killed his own mother, Steve had to give in to his urges and kill as well. So, he attacked the Carpenter family. That was why those two killings were different."

"And, in a way, that was what the son wanted too, right? For his dad to resurface. To bond with him in a sick sort of way."

I nodded. "Parker copied it down to the smallest detail, and he could do that because he had the book. He even knew about the daisies…even though…no one else had…"

I paused and looked out the window again as an idea shaped in my mind. I shook my head. No, it was nothing.

That was when the phone rang. Weasel took it as a signal to leave me and gave me a smile and a *keep up the good work*, then disappeared down the hallway while I picked up my phone.

"Ryder."

"Hello, this is Judy Marsh from the courthouse.

You called earlier in the week and asked about a name change. From back in seventy-four?"

It took me a second to remember what she was talking about, but then I did. "Oh, yes, the name change. Hello, Mrs. Marsh, thank you for calling me back."

"Well, it wasn't easy to find; that's why it took some time. Not just because it was a long time ago, and I had to go through all the archives for that year, but mostly because it was the wrong year. Steve Carver didn't change his name till nineteen-seventy-six. So, I was looking in all the wrong files."

I leaned forward. "But you found it? You know his new name?"

"I sure do," she said.

My heart pounded loudly in my chest while I listened, and Mrs. Marsh told me what she had found out. As I hung up and stared at the name I had jotted down on the notepad in front of me, I kept shaking my head.

"I'll be damned," I mumbled while fixating my eyes on it, letting the realization sink in, making sure I was seeing things right. It suddenly all made a lot of sense.

CHAPTER SIXTY-NINE

August 2018

She was turning the key over and over again, but the car wouldn't start. Her hands were getting clammy as Dennis plunged toward her car and now stood in front of it, grinning widely as the car once again coughed, then gave up.

"Come on, please," she whimpered.

Dennis slammed his hand onto her car, then laughed and approached her.

"Oh, dear God," she mumbled, trying to start the car again, but it still refused to obey.

Outside the window, she watched him come closer, then looked at her purse in the passenger seat next to her. She had never held a gun between her hands before.

Dennis was now by her door. Diane managed to lock it before he grabbed the handle and pulled it. In frustration, he slammed his hands against the window.

"Come out here, you bitch. I need to talk to you."

Diane looked at the purse again, her heart pounding in her chest. Could she shoot him if she had to? Would she be able to?

As he pulled the handle again, she reached over with a loud whimper and tried to grab the gun when she spotted a police car in her rearview mirror. Her eyes grew wide, and she forgot all about the gun as the car drove up behind her and stopped.

"Help," she screamed. "Help me, please."

Seeing the car, Dennis stopped pulling the handle of the car and stood up straight. The officer stepped out. Diane watched it all in the rearview mirror and could see the officer come closer.

"Thank you, God," she mumbled. "Thank you."

Diane stayed in the car and watched from the side view mirror how the officer approached Dennis and stopped outside of the back door of the car. Dennis approached him.

"Thank you for coming, Officer; she locked

herself inside the car...Wait a minute," she heard Dennis say.

Diane looked in the side view mirror and saw the officer pull out his gun, then fire it. With a gasp, she watched Dennis's body fall to the asphalt.

Did he just shoot Dennis? Oh, dear God, he did. He shot Dennis!

Diane hardly breathed. Panic rushed through her body. She moved and tried to get a better look at what was going on outside her car when the officer approached her window. He bent down and looked directly in at her.

The face was covered with a doll's mask, the mask picturing a woman with rosy red lips, light pink skin, and black painted eyebrows. The mask had deep holes where the eyes peeked out. Big steel-grey eyes.

Like those of a wolf.

CHAPTER SEVENTY

August 2018

I was calling her frantically while racing up A1A toward the north side of town. But Diane wasn't picking up.

"Come on, Diane. Pick up, pick up, pick up, please."

When she didn't, I threw the phone on the passenger seat next to me with a groan. I slammed my hand onto the steering wheel, scolding myself.

"Why didn't you go yourself? She called you. She needed your help. And you sent a lion to tend the sheep. How could you have been so stupid?"

I should have known it when he had started to talk about the daisies. I should have figured it out back then. Why hadn't I? Because it was too darn crazy to believe. But it made sense. It made a lot of sense. He was the only one who knew about the flowers. No one else did. It wasn't in any of the reports. I couldn't understand why it wasn't in any of the files, but now I understood. He was bragging, letting me know how superior he was.

The bastard.

I should have recognized him when looking at the old pictures of Steve Carver. I should have recognized the eyes, even the height that was so unusual, but I didn't because I could never have imagined it being him. It was too crazy to fathom. The guy had been fooling us for ages. Forty years on the force. Forty years he had been keeping a close eye on all of us, knowing as much as we did, knowing every move the police made. That was how he had stayed out of the spotlight. That was how he stayed under the radar.

Because he was one of us.

Dang it, Mike. I loved you, man. You were the nicest guy around. Why did it have to be you? Why?

I raced into Suwannee Lane, ignoring every red light and stop sign on the way, my sirens blaring from the car. I wanted him to know I was coming for him. I wanted him to understand that I knew. I had figured him out. He was never going to fool me again. Never.

As I raced up the street, I spotted Diane's car parked outside of her house. Behind it was one of our patrol cars. And there was Mike. He was wearing a mask, but I would recognize him anywhere. He was standing over a dead body on the ground, bent down by Diane's window, slamming his baton into the glass.

CHAPTER SEVENTY-ONE

August 2018

The glass splintered and flew everywhere. Diane managed to close her eyes but felt the splinters tear at her skin on her face and her arm. She screamed and threw herself to the side, trying to get to the gun. The officer reached inside and grabbed her arm with his gloved hand. Then she screamed. Diane screamed with all she had while the officer unlocked the car with the other hand and opened the door, then pulled her out onto the asphalt, her skin getting cut by the broken glass.

"Stop," she screamed. "Stop it."

She was thrown onto the ground before he pulled off his belt and wrapped it around her neck, tightening it so much that she had to gasp to breathe. Diane could hear the sound of another car stopping, and then someone yelling, but she had no idea what was going on. She felt the belt tighten around her throat and soon she couldn't breathe at all.

"Stop it," a voice said. "Please, Mike."

In her dizziness, she recognized it.

Jack?

"Don't get any closer," Mike said. "Or I'll kill her. I'll tighten the belt just enough. You won't be able to make it over here in time. Trust me. I have a lot of experience with these things. I know exactly how much pressure I need to add to close the deal. I have years of practice."

Diane managed to open her eyes while gasping for air, just enough to see Jack standing a few steps away, holding a gun pointed toward Mike, who was now taking off the mask.

She felt like her head was about to explode. Mike's massive body was holding her down.

"I prefer plastic bags, you know?" Mike said looking at her. "But this way is slower. This is just like when I killed my father. My first kill. Something so perfect about it, isn't there?"

"Stop it, Mike. You don't have to do this," Jack said.

"See, that's where you're wrong," Mike said. "So terribly wrong. I do have to do this. I do have to kill. For so many years, I was able to keep my desire at bay; I was able to live almost like a normal guy, only killing now and then when I could get away with it in the line of duty. But I knew it was bound to happen again. I was certain it would have happened when I was married to Amber. I was so sure I was going to kill her because she deserved it more than anyone. But it was too risky. It would have attracted way too much attention to me. So, I couldn't. But I dreamt of doing it; oh, how I dreamt of it, so many times. Instead, I walked away. I only spent a few years with her before I could tell it wasn't going to end well. And then, years later, my son did it. I cried when I saw it. It was so beautiful. The son completed what his father never managed to do. Made the old man proud. After that, I couldn't hold back. But I was rusty and needed a practice kill, so I spotted Mrs. Carpenter and just went for it. But my real fantasy was this one. Returning to where it all began. To close the circle. I stalked her for weeks and entered her house when she wasn't there or when she slept at night. I laid in her bed. I sent her the flowers while dreaming about how I was going to do it."

Diane closed her eyes again and focused on not panicking. She felt like all the blood in her body was stuck in her head. She was wheezing and pulling at every bit of air she could get through.

She felt Mike's hand tighten the belt further and finally gave up the fight. As she sunk into the ocean of stars, she could barely hear the shot blast through the air and she no longer cared.

CHAPTER SEVENTY-TWO

August 2018

Mike fell down on the asphalt. My heart stopped as I watched the guy I had once believed to be my friend sink lifeless to the ground.

I had shot him in the head. It took me a few seconds to gather the courage to, but it was the only way out. At first, I thought about going for the shoulder or the leg but knowing Mike, that wouldn't have stopped him. He was a big guy, six-foot-eight, and as tough as they get. And he had a gun of his own. I couldn't risk him going for that.

But it hurt like nothing else in this world.

I hurried to Diane. I grabbed the belt strap and loosened it. Still, Diane wasn't breathing. I bent down and performed CPR on her small, fragile body. Still, nothing happened.

"Come on, Diane," I said, weeping. "Please, breathe. Please."

I pressed her chest rhythmically, then blew air into her mouth, then back to pressing, while tears were streaming across my cheeks.

"Please, Diane."

Please, don't' tell me I hesitated too long.

It would end up destroying me if I had. I knew it would. There was no way I could live with myself if I hadn't reacted in time.

"Come on!"

I pressed her chest again and again until she finally took in a breath. I called for assistance over my radio, and soon the paramedics arrived and took over. I sank to the ground as I watched them work, and more cars arrived. I sat on the sidewalk and couldn't stop crying when I felt a hand on my shoulder and looked up.

Weasel gave me a sympathetic look. She nodded toward Mike's body on the asphalt not far from me.

"I'm guessing you have one hell of a story to tell me, am I right?"

I could only answer with a nod.

EPILOGUE

October 2018

I was holding the envelope tightly in my hand as I walked up the stairs, a rush of excitement going through my body. Downstairs, I could hear the kids playing in the living room while a thunderstorm raged outside.

Shannon was with them, and they were playing hide and go seek with the puppy—which we had named Molly. She was barking loudly and revealing where everyone was. I stopped for a second as I heard Abigail shriek when she was found, and I heard Shannon laugh loudly.

She was better. A lot better. After I had shot Mike and given Weasel my testimony, I had gone directly back to the motel and found her in one of the rooms. She had looked up at me with such deep sadness and guilt; it had torn my heart to pieces. I had walked directly to her, taken her into my arms, and kissed her deeply and lovingly the way I used to. I had cried and looked into her eyes and told her I loved her and that I never wanted to lose her and that she had scared me senseless getting high the way she did.

And then we talked. Four hours straight, we talked about everything. She told me how much pain she had been in and how she hadn't wanted to tell me because she didn't want me to worry and was probably scared I would tell her to stop the tour because of it, which she was probably right about.

We cried, we kissed, we talked, and we laughed. And we were back to being us again. Honest and with no more facades, no more lies. I told her honestly how seeing Diane again had awoken some old feelings in me, but also that I had realized those feelings weren't nearly as profound and important to me as the ones I had for my wife. The woman who had given me so much, the woman I shared a family with and so many children we could hardly count them anymore.

Shannon told me it made her sad to know that I had felt those emotions again for another woman, but that she understood. She also told me she had been terrified that I was replacing her, and I then told her Diane could never come anywhere close to replacing her. There was no way.

Then we kissed some more, and we agreed that Shannon was going to stay home and not do the rest of her tour. She was going to stop taking the pills and never touch anything like them again. Touring and playing concerts far away would have to wait until the kids were older and the pressure wasn't as tough. She needed to take care of herself first and foremost. And she needed to be with her family.

And then there was one more thing that I wanted. It was going to take her help, and, hopefully, my mom's as well. And maybe Sarah's, but we both agreed it was the right thing to do. As soon as Shannon was completely free from the pills and felt ready for it, it was going to happen.

And that moment had arrived now, a little more than a month later. She was ready she had told me, and now I had made the arrangements.

I walked down the hallway, thinking about Diane and how happy I was that she had moved to Tampa as soon as she was out of the hospital. She was going to sell the house, later on, she had told me, but she didn't want to be here in Cocoa Beach anymore. It was a great relief to me because I wanted to focus on my family now and, even though she was no threat, I knew Shannon saw her as one.

I stood for a few seconds in front of the door, finding the courage to knock. Then I did. A small voice answered.

"What?"

I opened the door and peeked inside. "Do you have a minute?"

Emily didn't even look at me. She seemed even smaller than she had the day before, and I felt a pinch in my stomach as I looked at her.

"What?" she asked and sat up.

I sat on the bed next to her, and she finally lifted her eyes and looked at me. I handed her the envelope, butterflies fluttering in my stomach.

"What's this?"

"Open it," I said.

"If it's something lame, Jack…"

"Just open it, will you?" I asked.

She did and pulled out something while wrinkling her forehead.

"What's this?"

"It's tickets," I said. "Two tickets. For the two of

us. To Bahamas. I've promised you we'd go since you were a little girl. I thought it was about time we did. Go find your family and meet them. Find out who you are. Where you come from."

Emily looked at me, her eyes wide, her mouth gaping.

"You're kidding me, right?"

I shook my head. "Nope. It's time, honey."

"And what about the kids?"

"Shannon says she'll take care of them. With a little help from grandma and Sarah, of course."

"And your work? Aren't you crazy busy?"

I shook my head. "Weasel let me have two weeks off. I figured it would be good for us. For you. The next two weeks are all about you. All my focus is on you."

Emily looked down at the tickets, then up at me, then down again. And then she smiled. For the first time in what felt like years, she smiled and, just like that, I once again felt hope that she was going to be all right. It was a small spark of hope, but it was all I had right now, and I was clinging to it like my life depended on it.

THE END

AFTERWORD

Dear Reader,

As you might know, this story was inspired by a real serial killer who went by the initials BTK for what he did to his victims—Bind, Torture, and Kill. He was known to break into people's houses and wait for them to come home. He roamed through the 70s then the 80s and wasn't caught until 2005. You can read more about him here, but I have to warn you, some of it is quite disturbing.

https://en.wikipedia.org/wiki/Dennis_Rader

https://www.kansas.com/news/special-reports/btk/article1003753.htmlB

It actually wasn't the killer himself that captured my attention in the first place. It was an article about people buying the houses many years later without knowing what had happened there. And once they found out, they were terrified. That was when a thought entered my mind: what if the killer returned? Or if someone else who was inspired by the killings did? And just like that, the story was born. I hope you enjoyed it and that you'll remember to lock your door from now on.

Especially on Monday mornings.

Take care,

Willow

ABOUT THE AUTHOR

The Queen of Scream, Willow Rose, is an international best-selling author. She writes Mystery/Suspense/Horror, Paranormal Romance and Fantasy. She is inspired by authors like James Patterson, Agatha Christie, Stephen King, Anne Rice, and Isabel Allende. She lives on Florida's Space Coast with her husband and two daughters. When she is not writing or reading, you'll find her surfing and watching the dolphins play in the waves of the Atlantic Ocean. She has sold more than three million books.

To be the first to hear about new releases and bargains—from Willow Rose—sign up below to be on the VIP List. (I promise not to share your email with anyone else, and I won't clutter your inbox.)

- Sign up to be on the VIP LIST here :

http://bit.ly/VIP-subscribe

Tired of too many emails? Text the word: “willowrose” to 31996 to sign up to Willow’s VIP text List to get a text alert with news about New Releases, Giveaways, Bargains and Free books from Willow.

Follow Willow Rose on BookBub:
https://www.bookbub.com/authors/willow-rose

Connect with Willow online:

- https://www.facebook.com/willowredrose
- www.willow-rose.net
- http://www.goodreads.com/author/show/4804769.Willow_Rose
- https://twitter.com/madamwillowrose
- madamewillowrose@gmail.com

WHAT HURTS THE MOST (7TH STREET CREW BOOK 1)

Excerpt

For a special sneak peak of Willow Rose's Bestselling Mystery Novel ***What hurts the most*** turn to the next page.

PROLOGUE

Cocoa Beach 1995

They're not going to let her go. She knows they won't. Holly is terrified as she runs through the park. The sound of the waves is behind her. A once so calming sound now brings utter terror to her. She is wet. Her shirt is dripping, her shoes making a slobbering sound as she runs across the parking lot towards the playground.

Run, run! Don't look back. Don't stop or they'll get you!

She can hear their voices behind her. It's hard to run when your feet are tied together. They're faster than she is, even though they are just walking.

"Oh, Holly," one of them yells. "Hoooollllyyy!"

Holly pants, trying to push herself forward. She

wants desperately to move faster, but the rope tied around her feet blocks them and she falls flat on her face onto the asphalt. Holly screams loudly as her nose scratches across the ground.

Get up! Get up and run. You can't let them get you.

She can hear them laughing behind her.

You can make it, Holly. Just get to A1A right in front of you. Only about a hundred feet left. There are cars on the road. They'll see you. Someone will see you and help you.

She tries to scream, but she has no air in her lungs. She is exhausted from swimming with her legs tied together. Luckily, her arms got free when she jumped in the water. They have pulled off her pants. Cut them open with a knife and pulled them off. Before they stabbed her in the shoulder. It hurts when she runs. Blood has soaked her white shirt. She is naked from the stomach down, except for her shoes and socks. Holly is in so much pain and can hardly move. Yet, she fights to get closer to the road.

A car drives by. Then another one. She can see them in the distance, yet her vision is getting foggier. She can't lose consciousness now.

You've got to keep fighting. You've got to get out of here! Don't give up, Holly. Whatever you do, just don't give up.

Their footsteps are approaching from behind.

Holly is groaning and fighting to get a few more steps in.

So close now. So close.

"Hurry up," she hears them yell. "She's getting away!"

Holly is so close now she can smell the cars' exhaust. All she needs to do is get onto the road, then stop a car. That's all she needs to do to get out of there alive. And she is so close now.

"Stop her, goddammit," a voice yells.

Holly fights to run. She moves her feet faster than she feels is humanly possible. She is getting there. She is getting there. She can hear them start to run now. They are yelling to each other.

"Shoot her, dammit."

Holly gasps, thinking about the spear gun. She's the one who taught them how to shoot it. She knows they won't hesitate to use it to stop her. She knows how they think. She knows this is what they do. She knows this is a kick for them, a drug.

She knows, because she is one of them.

"Stop the bitch!" someone yells, and she hears the sound of the gun going off. She knows this sound so well, having been spearfishing all her life and practiced using the gun on land with her father. He taught her everything about spearfishing, starting when she was no more than four years old. He even taught her to hold her breath underwater for a very long time.

"Scuba diving is for tourists. Real fishers free dive," she hears his voice say, the second the spear whistles through the air.

It hits Holly in the leg and she tumbles to the ground. Holly falls to the pavement next to A1A with a scream. She hears giggles and voices behind her. But she can also hear something else. While she drags herself across the pavement, she can hear the sound of sirens.

"Shit!" the voices behind her say.

"We gotta get out of here."

"RUN!"

CHAPTER ONE

September 2015

Blake Mills is enjoying his coffee at Starbucks. He enjoys it especially today. He is sipping it while looking at his own painting that they have just put up on display inside the shop. He has been trying to convince the owner of the local Starbucks in Cocoa Beach for ages to put up some of his art on display, and finally Ray agreed to let him hang up one of his turtle paintings. Just for a short period, to see how it goes.

It is Blake's personal favorite painting and he hopes it will attract some business his way. As a small artist in a small town, it is hard to make a living, even though Blake offers paintings by order, so anyone can get one any way they want it and can be sure it will fit their house or condo. It isn't exactly the way the life of an artist is supposed to be, but it is the only way to do it if he wants to eat.

Blake decides to make it a day of celebration and buys an extra coffee and a piece of cake to eat as well. He takes a bite and enjoys the taste.

"Looking good," a voice says behind him. He turns in his chair and looks into the eyes of Olivia.

Olivia Hartman. The love of his life.

Blake smiles to himself. "You came," he whispers and looks around. Being married, Olivia has to be careful whom she is seen with in this town.

"Can I sit?" she asks, holding her own coffee in her hand.

Blake pulls out a chair for her and she sits next to him. Blake feels a big thrill run through his body. He loves being with Olivia and has never had the pleasure of doing so in public. They usually meet up at his studio and have sex between his paintings on the floor or up against the wall. He has never been to her place on Patrick Air Force Base, where she lives with her husband, a general in the army. Blake is terrified of him and a little of her as well, but that is part of what makes it so wonderfully exciting. At the age of twenty-three, Blake isn't ready to settle down with anyone, and he isn't sure he is ever going to be. It isn't his style. He likes the carefree life, and being an artist he can't exactly provide for a family anyway. Having children will only force him to forget his dreams and get a *real job*. It would no doubt please his father, but Blake doesn't want a real job. He doesn't want the house on the water or the two to three children. He isn't cut out for it, and his many girlfriends in the past never understood that. All of them thought they could change him, that they were the one who could make him realize that he wanted it all. But he really didn't. And he still doesn't.

"It looks really great," Olivia says and sips her coffee. She is wearing multiple finger rings and bracelets, as always. She is delicate, yet strong. Used to be a fighter pilot in the army. Blake thought that was so cool. Today, she no longer works, not since she married the general.

She and Blake had met at the Officer's Club across the street from the base. He was there with a girl he had met at Grills in Cape Canaveral, who worked on base doing some contracting or something boring like that; she had invited him to a party. It was by far the most boring affair until he met Olivia on the porch standing with a beer in her hand overlooking the Atlantic Ocean. She was slightly tipsy and they exchanged pleasantries for a few minutes before she turned and looked at him with that mischievous smile of hers. Then she asked him if he wanted to have some fun.

"Always," he replied.

They walked to the beach and into the dunes, where they enjoyed the best sex of Blake's life.

Now it has become a drug to him. He needs his fix. He needs her.

"Congrats," she says.

"Thanks. Now I just hope someone will grab one of the business cards I've put on the counter and call me to order a painting. I could use the money. I only had one order last month."

"They will," she says, laughing. "Don't you worry about that." She leans over and whispers through those pouty lips of hers. "Now let's go back to your place and celebrate."

"Is that an order?" he asks, laughing.

"Is that an order, *ma'am*," she corrects him. "And, yes, it is."

CHAPTER TWO

September 2015

Being with Olivia is exhilarating. It fills him with the most wonderful sensation in his body because Blake has never met anyone like her, who can make him crazy for her. Not like this. But at the same time, it is also absolutely petrifying because she is married to General Hartman, who will have Blake killed if he ever finds out. There is no doubt about it in Blake's mind.

Yet, he keeps sleeping with her. Even though he keeps telling himself it is a bad idea, that he has to stop, that it is only a matter of time before he will get himself in some deep shit trouble. Blake knows it is bad to be with her. He knows it will get him in trouble eventually, but still, he can't help himself.

He has to have her. He has to taste her again and again. No matter the cost.

Their lips meet inside Blake's studio as soon as they walk in. Blake closes his eyes and drinks from her. He doesn't care that the door behind him is left open. Nothing else matters right now.

"I thought you couldn't get out today," he says, panting, when her lips leave his. "Isn't the general on base?"

"He is," she mumbles between more kisses.

It has been two weeks since they were together last. Two weeks of constantly dreaming and longing for her. They communicate via Snapchat. It is untraceable, as far as Blake knows. Blake wrote a message to her a few days ago, telling her about the painting being put up in Starbucks, knowing that she probably couldn't come and see it. He even sent a picture of the painting. It is also her favorite. She messaged him back a photo of her sad face telling him she didn't think she could get out, since her husband was home. Usually, she only dares to meet with Blake when her husband is travelling. Even then, they have to be extremely careful. General Hartman has many friends in Cocoa Beach and his soldiers are seen everywhere.

"I told him I was seeing a friend today. It's not

like it's a lie. I don't care anymore if he finds out about us. I'm sick of being just the general's wife. I want a life of my own."

Blake takes off his T-shirt and her hands land on his chest. He rips off her shirt and several buttons fall to the floor. She closes her eyes and moans at his touches. His hands cup her breasts and soon her bra lands on the wooden floor. He grabs her hair and pulls her head back while kissing her neck. His heart is pumping in his chest just from the smell of her skin.

"You can't," he whispers between breaths. "You can't let him know about us. He'll kill the both of us."

Olivia lets out a gasp as Blake reaches up under her skirt and places a hand in her panties, and then rips them off. He pushes her up against a table, then lifts her up, leans over her naked torso and puts his mouth to her breasts. He closes his eyes and takes in her smell, drinking the juices of her body, then pulls his shorts down and gently slides inside of her with a deep moan. She puts her legs around his neck, partly strangling him when she comes in pulsing movements back and forth, her body arching.

"Oh, Blake…oh, Blake …"

The sensation is burning inside of him and he is

ready to explode. Olivia is moaning and moving rapidly. His movements are urgent now, the intensity building. He is about to burst, when suddenly she screams loudly and pushes him away. Blake falls to the floor with a thud.

"What the…?"

Blake soon realizes why Olivia is screaming and feels the blood rush from his face. A set of eyes is staring down at him.

The eyes of Detective Chris Fisher.

"Blake Mills, you're under arrest," the voice belonging to the eyes says.

CHAPTER THREE

September 2015

"I'm sorry, Mary, there's nothing I can do."

I stare at my boss, Chief Editor, Markus Fergusson. He is leaning back in his leather chair in his office on the twenty-eighth floor of the Times-Tower on the west side of mid-town. Behind him, the view is spectacular, but I hardly notice anymore. After five years working there, you simply stop being baffled. However, I am actually baffled at this moment. But not because of the view. Because of what is being said.

"So, you're firing me, is that it?" I ask, while my blood is boiling in my veins. What the hell is this?

"We're letting you go, yes."

"You can't do that, Markus, come on. Just because of this?"

He leans over his desk and gives me that look that I have come to know so well in my five years as a reporter for *The New York Times*.

"Yes."

"I don't get it," I say. "I'm being fired for writing the paper's most read article in the past five years?"

Markus sighs. "Don't put up a fight, will you? Just accept it. You violated the rules, sweetheart."

Don't you sweetheart me, you pig!

"I don't make the rules, Mary. The big guys upstairs make the decisions and it says here that we have to let you go for *violating the normal editing process.*"

I squint my eyes. I can't believe this. "I did what?"

"You printed the story without having a second set of eyes on it first. The article offended some people, and, well…"

He pauses. I scoff. He is such a sell-out. Just because my article didn't sit well with some people, some influential people, he is letting me go? They want to fire me for some rule bullshit?

"Brian saw it," I say. "He read it and approved it."

"The rules say *two* editors," he says. "On a story

like this, this controversial, you need two editors to approve it, not just one."

"That's BS and you know it, goddammit, Markus. I never even heard about this rule. What about Brian?"

"We're letting him go as well."

"You can't do that! The man just had another kid."

Markus shrugs. "That's not really my problem, is it? Brian knew better. He's been with us for fifteen years."

"It was late, Markus. We had less than five minutes to deadline. There was no time to get another approval. If we'd waited for another editor, the story wouldn't have run, and you wouldn't have sold a record number of newspapers that day. The article went viral online. All over the world. Everyone was talking about it. And this is how you thank me?"

I rise from the chair and grab my leather jacket. "Well, suit yourself. It's your loss. I don't need you or this paper."

I leave, slamming the door, but it doesn't make me feel as good as I thought it would. I pack my things in that little brown box that they always do in the movies and grab it under my arm before I leave in the elevator. On the bottom floor, I hand in my ID card to the guard in the lobby and Johnson looks at me with his mouth turned downwards.

"We'll miss you, Miss Mary," he says.

"I'll miss you too, Johnson," I say, and walk out the glass doors, into the streets of New York without a clue as to what I am going to do. Living in Manhattan isn't cheap. Living in Manhattan with a nine-year old son, as a single mom isn't cheap at all. The cost for a private school alone is over the roof.

I whistle for a cab, and before I finally get one, it starts to rain, and I get soaked. I have him drive me back to my apartment and I let myself inside. Snowflake, my white Goldendoodle is waiting on the other side of the door, jumping me when I enter. He licks me in my face and whimpers from having missed me since I left just this morning. I sit down on my knees and pet him till he calms down. I can't help smiling when I am with him. I can't feel sad for long when he's around. It's simply not possible. He looks at me with those deep brown eyes.

"We'll be alright, won't we, Snowflake? I'm sure we will. We don't need them, no we don't."

CHAPTER FOUR

September 2015

"Do you come here often?"

Liz Hester stares at the man who has approached her in the bar at Lou's Blues in Indialantic. It is Friday night and she was bored at the base, so she and her friends decided to go out and get a beer.

"You're kidding me, right?"

The guy smiles. He is a surfer-type with long greasy hair under his cap, a nice tan, and not too much between the ears. The kind of guy who opens each sentence with *dude,* even when speaking to a girl.

"It was the best I could come up with."

"You do realize that I am thirty-eight and you're at least fifteen years younger, right?"

Kim comes up behind her. She is wearing her blue ASU—army service uniform—like Liz. They are both decorated with several medals. Liz's includes the Purple Heart, given to her when she was shot during her service in Afghanistan. Took a bullet straight to her shoulder. The best part was, she took it for one of her friends. She took it for Britney, who is also with them this night, hanging out with some guy further down the bar. They are friends through thick and thin. Will lay down their lives for one another.

Liz's eyes meet those of Jamie's across the bar. She smiles and nods in the direction of the guy that Liz is talking to. Liz smiles and nods too. There is no need for them to speak; they know what she is saying.

He's the one.

"So, tell me, what's your name?" Liz asks the guy. She is all of a sudden flirtatious, smiling and touching his arm gently. Kim giggles behind her, but the guy doesn't notice.

"I'm Billy. My friends call me Billy the Kid."

"Well, you are just a kid, aren't you?" she says, purring like a cat, leaning in over the bar.

The guy lifts his cap a little, then puts it back on. "You sure are a lot of woman."

Liz knows his type. He is one of those who gets aroused just by looking at a woman in uniform. She has met her share of those types. They are a lot of fun to play with.

"Well, maybe I can make a man of you," she whispers, leaning very close to his face.

The guy laughs goofily. "You sure can," he says and gives her an elevator look. "I sure wouldn't mind that. I got an anaconda in my pants you can ride if you like."

Liz laughs lightly, and then looks at Jamie again, letting her know he has taken the bait.

"Well, why don't you—Billy the Kid—meet me outside in the parking lot in say—five minutes?"

Billy laughs again. "Dude! Whoa, sure!"

Billy taps the bar counter twice, not knowing exactly what to do with himself, then lifts his cap once again and wipes sweat off his forehead. He has nice eyes, Liz thinks, and he is quite handsome.

As stupid as they get, though.

He leaves her, shooting a finger-gun at her and winking at the same time. The girls approach Liz, moving like cats sliding across the floor. Liz finishes her drink while the four of them stick their heads together.

"Ready for some fun?" she asks.

They don't say anything. They don't have to.

CHAPTER FIVE

September 2015

She waits for him by the car. Smoking a cigarette, she leans against it, blowing out smoke when she spots him come out of the bar and walk towards her. Seeing the goofy grin on his face makes her smile even wider.

"Hey there, baby," Billy says and walks up to her. "I have to say, I wasn't sure you would even be here. A nice lady like you with a guy like me? You're a wild cat, aren't you?"

Liz chuckles and blows smoke in his face. "I sure am."

Billy the Kid moves his body in anticipation. His crotch can't keep still. He is already hard.

What a sucker.

He looks around with a sniffle. "So, where do

you want to go? To the beach? Or do you…wanna do it right here…?" he places a hand next to her on the car. "Up against this baby, huh?"

Liz laughs again, then leans closer to him till her mouth is on his ear. "You're just full of yourself, aren't you?"

"What?" he asks with another goofy grin.

"Did you really think you were going to get lucky with me? With this?" She says and points up and down her body.

The grin is wiped off his face. Finally.

"What is this?" he asks, his face in a frown. "Were you just leading me on? What a cunt!" He spits out the last word. He probably means it as an insult, but Liz just smiles from ear to ear as her friends slowly approach from all sides, surrounding Billy. When he realizes, he tries to back out, but walks into Jamie and steps on her black shoes.

"Hey, those are brand new! Dammit!"

Jamie pushes him in the back forcefully and he is now in the hands of Britney. Britney is smaller than the others, but by far the strongest. She clenches her fist and slams it into his face. The blow breaks his nose on the spot and he falls backwards to the asphalt, blood running from it.

"What the…what…who are you?" Billy asks, disoriented, looking from woman to woman.

"We like to call ourselves the Fast and the Furious," Liz says.

"Yeah, cause I'm fast," Kim says and kicks Billy in the crotch. He lets out a loud moan in pain.

The sound is almost arousing to Liz.

"And I'm furious," she says, grabbing him by the hair and pulling his head back. She looks him in the eyes. She loves watching them squirm, the little suckers. Just like she loved it back in Afghan when she interrogated the *Haji*.

Haji is the name they call anyone of Arab decent, or even of a brownish skin tone. She remembers vividly the first time they brought one in. It was the day after she had lost a good friend to an IED, a roadside bomb that detonated and killed everyone in the truck in front of her. They searched for those suckers all night, and finally, the next morning they brought in three. Boy, she kicked that sucker till he could no longer move. Hell, they all did it. All of them let out their frustrations. Losing three good soldiers like that made them furious. Liz was still furious. Well, to be frank, she has been furious all of her life.

Everybody around her knows that.

Liz laughs when she hears Billy's whimper, then uses two fingers to poke his eyes forcefully. Billy screams.

"My eyes, my eyes!"

Liz lets go of his hair and looks at her girls. They are all about to burst in anticipation. She opens the door to the car, where Jamie has placed a couple of bottles of vodka to keep them going all night. She lets out a loud howl like a wolf, the girls chiming in, then lifts Billy the Kid up and throws him in the back of the Jeep.

End of excerpt...

ORDER YOUR COPY TODAY!

CLICK HERE TO ORDER:

https://readerlinks.com/l/157401

Made in the USA
Middletown, DE
03 February 2023

23877511R00250